D0983926

THE SPACE SHIP IN THE PARK

THE SPACE SHIP IN THE PARK

LOUIS SLOBODKIN

THE MACMILLAN COMPANY, New York, New York
COLLIER-MACMILLAN LTD., London

The Macmillan Company, 866 Third Avenue, New York, N.Y. 10022
Collier-Macmillan Canada Ltd., Toronto, Ontario
Library of Congress catalog card number: 70–187799
Printed in the United States of America

1 2 3 4 5 6 7 8 9 10

Contents

1	*Three Strange Calls*	1
2	*The Flying Ice-Cream Cart*	13
3	*The Interplanetary Explorers*	33
4	*Klunko . . . Junko!*	50
5	*Cyfarchiad Dieidhryn*	71
6	*Magic Dust*	91
7	*The Search*	102
8	*Silver Noses*	121
9	*Source of the Secret Power*	135
10	*The Message on the Moon*	148
11	*On the Stoop*	165

THE SPACE SHIP IN THE PARK

1. Three Strange Calls

THIS was the summer that Eddie Blow was not going to spend his vacation at his grandmother's apple farm on a mountainside up above Albany, New York. Right after school finished Eddie was going to get a job!

He was going to work in the playground near his school. He was going to help keep things in order and help the man who had charge of the playground.

But somehow that is not what happened. School ended and Eddie did not get the job. An old man was hired to do the work in the playground that Eddie and five other boys were going to do. And since Eddie was not going to spend his vacation on his grandmother's farm, she went to visit her cousin Matilda who lived on the other side of the mountain in a tiny house too small for more than two people.

Eddie had no place to go for his vacation. So he hung around the streets and the small apartment in New York City where he lived with his mother. Or he went to the library or the Natural History Museum (Eddie was always interested in science and nature study). Sometimes he went to Central Park with his Boy Scout troop.

He often thought about how pleasant and cool it was on his grandmother's farm during the summer. He thought of the creek where he fished and swam . . . the barn . . . the places where he hiked.

Yes, Eddie expected this was going to be a very dull summer in the city until the day he received a very strange telephone call!

In fact, it was a day when there were three strange telephone calls. His mother answered the first call when the telephone rang. She told Eddie later that just as the telephone rang the electric light in the kitchen (which was always lit—it was a dark kitchen) flashed on and off in the strangest way. Eddie was down on the street hanging around the stoop and talking to some boys at the time.

His mother told Eddie later, "It was the strangest thing, Eddie. After that telephone rang and the lights flashed on

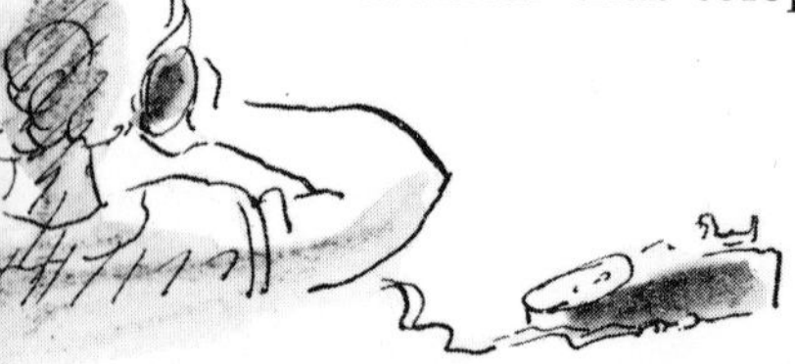

and off I answered it and all I could hear was a crackling like radio static or maybe like a forest fire. Then a roaring, swish-swish sound like something going at tremendous speed—but no one said anything so I hung up."

After a while the phone rang again. Eddie's mother answered it again and at first heard the strange crackling, roaring, swishing sounds. Then they cleared away. And she heard someone at the other end say:

"Ed-die!"

It was a sharp, high-pitched voice with a foreign accent, it seemed to her. She thought perhaps it might be Russian or Hungarian.

"Oh, you want Eddie?" she said into the mouthpiece. "One moment, please, I'll call him."

She put her head out the window and called down to Eddie sitting on the front stoop.

"Oh, Eddie . . . Eddie!"

He did not hear her. He was in the middle of explaining jet propulsion in space ships again to a little boy who always forgot about such things.

"Hey, Eddie, your ma's calling," said Eddie's best friend, Willie Jackson. "She's looking out the window."

"Yes, ma'am, do you want me?" shouted Eddie.

"There's someone on the telephone asking for you," said his mother.

"I'll be right up. See you later, Willie," said Eddie. He tapped the little boy on the head and bounded up the stairs.

When he got to the phone he put the receiver to his ear and said:

"Hello. Hello. This is Eddie. Who is this?"

There was no answer. Whoever it was was gone. There was no one on the other end of the phone.

"Oh, well. They'll phone back again," said his mother. "Eddie, do you know any Russians or Hungarians? The voice of that person who asked for you must have been from . . ."

Then the phone rang again for the third time. Eddie grabbed the phone.

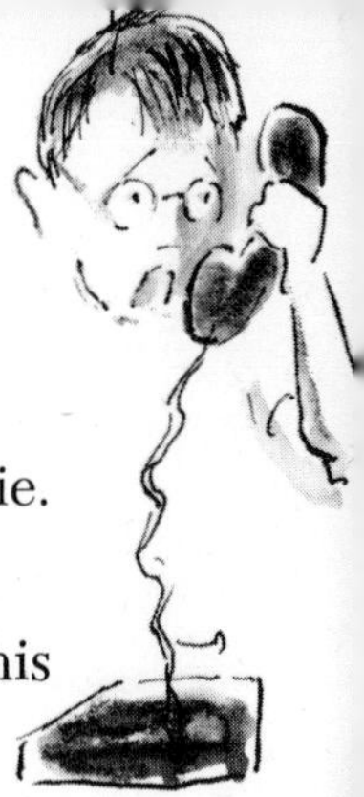

"Hello. Hello," he shouted into the receiver.

"Talk quiet," said a voice at the other end. "Ed-die?"

"Yeh, this is . . . Oh, hey, is this Marty?" shouted Eddie. "Marty, where are . . ."

Eddie interrupted himself to explain to his mother, "This is a friend of mine. Hey, Marty, say, what d'ya know?"

From the other end Marty repeated sternly, "Talk quiet. Listen . . . meet in Park Central in animal zoo near kangaroo . . . four P.M."

"You mean you're here, Marty . . . here in New York . . . in the zoo?"

At the other end there was a click.

Marty's voice stopped talking and Eddie heard the roaring, swishing, swooshing, crackling sounds his mother had heard. Eddie hung up the receiver.

For a moment Eddie was bewildered.

Then he looked at his wristwatch (with the compass on the back) and said, "It's two minutes to four. I'm gonna meet a friend over in the park, Mom."

And Eddie ran out the door and down the stairs.

His mother called after him, "Eddie, do be careful crossing streets. Please don't run. And don't stay in the park too late. Remember supper."

Eddie slowed up a bit and as he went down the rest of the stairs he thought, Now what could Marty be doing here . . .

here in Central Park? (That, of course, was what he meant by Park Central.) How did he know our number? What was that strange, roaring, crackling sound on the telephone? It sounded like static out of a giant radio. Where was Marty speaking from?

The reason Eddie asked himself so many questions about his friend Marty was that Marty was not just an ordinary friend . . . a regular boy Eddie knew, like his friend Willie Jackson, his next-door neighbor. No, Marty was most irregular. Marty was a boy from outer space! Eddie had met Marty on his grandmother's farm a few summers ago!

Marty was a Junior Scientist Explorer from the planet Martinea and he had his own space ship! In fact, Eddie had been up in Marty's space ship. Perhaps Marty was speaking from his space ship as he raced to Central Park from Martinea.

Eddie reached the bottom of the long flight of stairs and came out on the front stoop.

"What you gotta do?" asked Willie as Eddie came down the steps. "What's your ma want you to do?"

"I don't have to do anything," said Eddie. "I've gotta go someplace."

"I'm doing nothing. Do you want me to go along?" asked Willie.

"We-ell." Eddie hesitated a moment. He had never told

anyone about Marty, that he was a Junior Scientist Explorer and that he could fly his space ship over 346,781 miles an hour, and things like that. He was sure no one would believe him. His grandmother, who knew Marty, just thought he was a nice boy . . . one of Eddie's friends.

Eddie's mother, of course, did not know Marty. And Eddie never told her about him. She would worry if she knew Eddie rode around with Marty in his space ship. She never flew on planes when she traveled, and never used the elevators in department stores. She rode on the escalator.

After a moment Eddie said to Willie, "Sure, come on along. I'm gonna meet a fellow I know. He's over in the Central Park Zoo . . . he called me on the telephone."

"How?" asked Willie after they'd walked a bit.

"How what?" said Eddie.

"How'd he call you in the zoo? There's no telephone booth in the zoo," said Willie.

"We-ell," said Eddie. He too knew there was no telephone booth in the zoo. But Marty did not need a telephone. He could arrange things. Right then and there as they waited for the traffic light to change from red (Don't Walk) to green (Walk), Eddie decided to tell his best friend, Willie, the truth about Marty.

"Willie," he said, "I'm gonna tell you something I never told anybody . . . a real big secret. Now you gotta promise . . ."

"Promise what? What secret?" asked Willie.

"Promise you'll never tell anyone what I tell you," said Eddie.

"O.K. I promise. What's the secret?"

"Scout's honor!" said Eddie grimly.

"Scout's honor," said Willie.

They shook hands with the secret Boy Scout shake.

"Now," said Eddie, after he looked around and lowered his voice to a hoarse whisper, "the fellow we're gonna meet in the park is a spaceman!"

"An astronaut!" yipped Willie.

"Shush! Not an astronaut . . . a spaceman! A man from outer space, I mean."

Willie's eyes widened and his mouth fell open in amazement. When he recovered he gasped.

"Na-aw!"

"Yes, he is," insisted Eddie, "and I was on his space ship and everything."

"On his space ship! Zowie!" howled Willie.

"Keep it down, will you?" whispered Eddie.

Then in the next few minutes, during the time it took them to dogtrot over to Central Park from Amsterdam Avenue where Eddie and Willie lived, Eddie told Willie a lot about Marty. He told how he first met him when Marty landed and hid his space ship in a gully under an apple tree on Eddie's grandmother's farm; about the time Marty and Eddie explored the United States in Marty's space ship; the time they went to London; the time Marty took Eddie along with a kangaroo and assorted animals to visit his own planet, the planet Martinea.

Again and again Eddie had to repeat, "Now Willie, this is absolutely true . . . it really happened," or something like that, because from the expression on Willie's face Eddie knew he was doubtful.

Fortunately, it was only two long blocks from Amsterdam Avenue to Central Park. (That's the reason Eddie's mother lived there. She liked the neighborhood so near the park.) Eddie was glad when they got into the park and they took a shortcut along the paths they knew to the zoo. They were narrow paths and they had to dogtrot single file. Eddie was relieved that he did not have to talk about Marty any more.

When they reached the zoo they quickly moved through the late-afternoon crowd to the caged runway that held the kangaroos and the wallabies.

There at an intersection of the paths in front of the kangaroos' runway stood Marty!

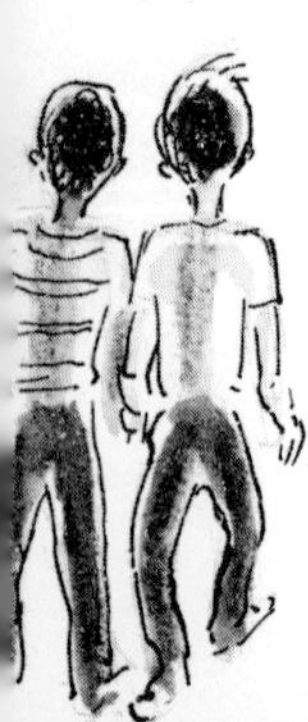

Eddie had seen Marty in many getups: his regular deep green Martinean spaceman's uniform with its many pockets; disguised as an ordinary American boy in a pair of Eddie's jeans (trouser legs rolled up like tires around his ankles—he was so much shorter than Eddie); dressed as a Cub Scout in Eddie's old Cub Scout shirt that flapped around his skinny figure; in his own Boy Scout shirt with the sleeves covered with merit badges from his wrists to his shoulders; then when he wore the shiny silk top hat in London.

The last time Eddie saw Marty he was dressed up in a pagoda-shaped hat from Hong Kong, a wraparound dia-

per from Bangkok, and flowered wreaths he got in Hawaii. And no matter what costume Marty wore he always wore his big non-gravity jet-propelled space shoes.

But Eddie was not prepared for the costume Marty wore this time. This time he was dressed up in a white jacket and cap and stood alongside an ice-cream cart!

Marty was disguised as a Good Humor ice-cream man!

2. The Flying Ice-Cream Cart

When Marty first saw Eddie coming along he grinned. But he frowned as soon as he realized that Eddie had brought Willie along to their secret meeting.

"Hey, Marty," shouted Eddie.

Marty just nodded and kept frowning as he looked at Willie.

"Oh, Marty, this is my friend Willie," said Eddie. "He's a First Class Scout." Then he whispered, "Willie can keep a secret too."

That softened up Marty at once. He grinned and reached out his hand. Willie and he shook hands with the secret

Boy Scout shake. Marty had learned about scouting from Eddie. He'd been to a Boy Scout Jamboree once and he had read an old Boy Scout *Manual* that Eddie had given him. He knew Scouts were trustworthy, honest, loyal, and all that.

"Marty, where's your . . ." Eddie was going to whisper "space ship," but he caught himself in time as two children, a girl and her little brother, stopped at the ice-cream cart.

The boy said, "Cho-co-lit."

And after a moment of thought his sister said, "I'd just like to have a toasted coconut pistachio ice-cream special with sprinkles, please. He wants the Eskimo Pie on a stick."

Marty the Good Humor man shrugged his shoulders.

"No more . . . all finished."

The children were very disappointed. The girl dragged her little brother away. He looked as if he was going to cry.

Then as three other little boys started to walk toward the ice-cream cart Marty grabbed the handle of the cart, twitched his head to Eddie and Willie to indicate they should follow him, and he went flying down the path, pushing the cart at a good clip.

Eddie and Willie ran after him. The three little boys with ice-cream ambitions were left far behind.

Marty, with his ice-cream cart, whirled down one path and up another, side-stepping anyone who looked as if he wanted to buy ice cream. At last he turned into a narrow lane, went through a hedge, and came to rest in a shaded dell in back of an old brick building that had once been the lion house.

Eddie and Willie followed him as quickly as they could go. Both of them were sweating and puffing after that fast chase. But Marty was calm and cool as he waited for them. Obviously, he had used one of his special speeds on his non-gravity shoes. Eddie knew that because he had seen Marty do it before. But Willie didn't. He just grinned and gasped.

"What a man!"

Marty twirled his head around and looked in all directions.

"Where man?" he asked quickly.

Eddie hastily explained, "Willie meant you went very fast."

Willie nodded and Marty was satisfied for a moment.

When Marty made his first trip to Earth from his planet Martinea he came prepared with his dictionary box, ready to translate English into his own language. He had studied English on Martinea with scientists who observed the billboards on the highways of the United States through powerful interplanetary telescopes. (They were not really telescopes, but that is the closest English translation we have for the Martinean name of the instrument, "Kookaufenvieten.")

With these examples of the English language, such as "Go slow, Bear right, Soft shoulder ahead, Stop, Turn Left, Welcome to Okachobee," they were able to reconstruct the English language. But Marty did carry a dictionary box as a precaution to help him with lesser-known words. It was evident he had no dictionary box with him this time.

"What a man . . . means go very fast?" asked Marty with raised eyebrows.

"Oh, Marty, it means Willie thinks you're pretty good . . . good and fast."

Marty smiled. "Good new non-gravity shoes," he explained to Willie. And he lifted his left foot to show off his shoe.

"Marty, where's your space ship?" asked Eddie to change the subject.

"Keep voice down," whispered Marty sternly. After looking around very carefully in all directions including up (since there might be some uninvited spy in the branches overhead) Marty called Eddie and Willie into a close huddle.

"Here is new invisible disguised space ship!"

"Where?"

Marty pointed directly at the ice-cream cart!

"No! No, Marty! That can't be!" exclaimed Eddie.

"Keep voice down," demanded Marty sharply. "Yes, can be . . . is! This space ship satellite disguised."

"Oh-h," said Eddie. He remembered that Marty's space ships on some of his previous visits to the planet Earth were disguised as little automobiles, the kind of European automobiles that Eddie had seen many times on the streets of New York. He thought they looked like overgrown peanut roasters.

"Put on visualizers," said Marty. He gave a pair of rose-colored glasses to Eddie and found another pair in one of his pockets and gave that one to Willie. Then he put a pair on himself.

Marty waved his hand toward the ice-cream cart. "Here is very latest modern Martinean satellite spaceship perambulator . . . travels in space over land, sea and air."

"Man . . . oh man . . . oh man . . . That's super duper," exclaimed Willie joyfully.

"It sure is," echoed Eddie, but he really did not think so.

This revealed space ship was much smaller than Marty's other space ships. This was Marty's fifth space ship and the others were not very big either.

"Marty, did you come all the way from Martinea in *that?*" asked Eddie.

"No, used new special interplanetary spacial Astro Rocket Space Ship. Now orbit around planet Earth. Wait for rendezvous. This only satellite of Astro Rocket Ship."

"What happened to that ice-cream cart?" Willie wanted to know.

"It's here," said Eddie.

"Where?"

"Right here in this space ship," said Eddie.

Then he went on to explain to the best of his ability Marty's space ships . . . what they were made of, how they were disguised and became invisible. Marty interjected a word now and then that tended to confuse Willie more rather than to clear things up for him.

"You see, Willie," began Eddie, "Marty's space ships are made of two bamboozelurgical metals developed in Martinea."

"This latest new metal," interrupted Marty. "Bamboozelurgical plus two."

"Yeah, plus two like he said," continued Eddie. "One metal resists all visual light rays and can only be seen with the visualizers we're wearing. That's the real space ship. The other metal is just a disguise. That's what the ice-cream cart is made of. It's a good strong metal visible without visualizers but it can fold up like paper if you want it to . . . and know how to fold it."

"Yeah," said Willie, still uncertain, "how'd you know all that?"

"Well, like I told you, Willie, I've seen Marty's space ships before. And he's given me rides on them," said Eddie.

"Inspect space ship?" asked Marty, with a polite wave of his hand.

"Hmm . . . not now," said Willie. "I've gotta get home for supper."

"Oh, Willie," said Eddie, "just one look can't hurt anything. Besides, Marty's space ships are as safe as . . . as . . . well, as a subway train or a bus. Come on, let's give it a quick look."

The space ship was shaped something like a Dutch

wooden shoe. It was topped by a transparent dome. Marty swung open a side door of the space ship and stepped into it. Eddie and Willie followed.

When Marty snapped the side door shut three seats sprang up from the floor of the space ship. In front of Marty there was a small instrument panel. Marty explained that that was all there was to the very latest modern Martinean satellite space-ship perambulator.

In the front of the space ship there was a concentrated storage of Secret Power ZZZ (Zupperior Zonetic Zurianomatichrome) plus one, which is the source of power used on all of Marty's spaceships. And in the rear, right in back of where they sat, there was a powerful diminutive jet engine with rockets that propelled the space ship so swiftly over land and sea (or rivers, ponds, and mudholes) and through space.

Of course, this little space ship could not fly long distances without refueling (only about 157,879 earth miles), but it was very efficient within its limitations.

"Would like small exploration?" asked Marty politely.

"No! . . . Not me!" said Willie. "I told you I gotta go. My mother expects me home for supper."

"Willie," said Eddie, "I gotta go home too. What time is it?" He looked at his wristwatch. "It's only ten minutes after four. Marty travels awfully fast . . ."

As Eddie was talking a park attendant came up the path pushing a wheelbarrow. He stopped and stared at them. Since he was not wearing visualizers he could not see the space ship. All he saw were three boys sitting or standing (he couldn't tell) in the middle of an ice-cream cart!

"Hey there," said the park attendant, "I thought those carts carried ice cream. It must be cold sitting in there . . . heh, heh. Well, we have had a hot day."

"It's his ice-cream cart," said Eddie, pointing to Marty.

"And I suppose you three are the cream of the crop," said the park attendant. "Heh, heh . . . that's a good one . . . ice cream of the crop. I gotta remember to tell . . ."

He had turned his back as he spoke. As soon as he said, "Remember to tell," Marty pushed the blast-off button on his instrument panel. There was a powerful rocket on the bottom of the space ship that propelled it straight up.

Then Marty pushed another button and the space ship stopped its quick ascent, and hovered about three miles above Central Park, over a bank of clouds.

"What happened?" yelped Willie.

"Oh, Marty, why did you do that?" asked Eddie.

Marty turned and with lifted eyebrows said, "You no hear man say he will 'tell' space-ship secret!"

That was the one thing that worried Marty most on all his visits to the planet Earth—that some grown-up would know and tell of his secret Martinean space ship.

"Marty, he wasn't going to tell about your space ship," said Eddie. "He was just gonna tell someone a joke."

"What is joke?" asked Marty.

"A joke," said Eddie, after a moment's thought, "is when you say something and you mean something else and people laugh . . . I guess that's what it is."

"When you say something, mean something else. This is not truth!" said Marty, his eyebrows climbing higher on his forehead. He believed the truth was very important to Boy Scouts.

"It's a joke, Marty. Anyway, I mean that man is not going to tell anybody about your space ship. He didn't even see it."

Marty knit his brow a moment, then nodded his head.

"Look, Marty," said Eddie, "can't we go on a short exploration, just to show Willie how your space ship works?"

"Space ship no work," said Marty stiffly, "space ship flies."

"I mean flies," said Eddie.

"Listen, man," said Willie, "I don't wanna go no place. I just wanna go back to Amsterdam Avenue."

"It won't take more than a couple of minutes," insisted Eddie. "Will it, Marty? We went all the way to London, England, last summer in just three minutes and two seconds. Didn't we, Marty?"

"Two minutes, three seconds," corrected Marty smugly. Then he turned to Willie. "Would like explore Canada Rocky Mountains?"

"Canadian Rocky Mountains?" exclaimed Willie.

"Maybe United States Rocky Mountains?" suggested Marty.

"Aw, Willie . . . it really will take just a few minutes, won't it, Marty?" said Eddie.

Marty consulted the instrument on his wrist that served him as a watch and he studied another instrument on his wrist to calculate the distance to the United States Rockies. Marty had already explored the United States very thoroughly.

"Fly to United States Rocky Mountains . . . return New York five minutes seven seconds," said Marty finally. "Satellite space-ship perambulator not fast like other space-ships."

"See, Willie, it's just five minutes and seven seconds to fly to the Rocky Mountains and back. We won't spend more than a few minutes looking at the Rockies and we'll come right back," said Eddie persuasively.

"Look, man! The only place I want to go back to is back to Amsterdam Avenue," insisted Willie.

While they talked Marty was fussing with his instrument door and automatic pilot chart, arranging his buttons

on the chart in case it finally was decided that they would go to the Rocky Mountains.

Suddenly the space ship was immersed in a bank of dark, clinging, wet clouds that had been pushed by a sudden gust of wind. Marty, who could not see the instrument board, made a wild jab just to push one of the buttons to get out of that dark enveloping cloud . . . ZIP . . . ZO-OM . . . SWOOP. They were off . . .

Marty had pushed the blast-off button.

"Next stop United States Rocky Mountains," announced Marty after he looked at the button he had pushed.

"Stop it! Turn around!" shouted Willie. "I gotta go home!"

Marty shook his head.

"No can do," said Marty.

He explained so that Eddie and Willie understood that on this space ship all long flight was automatic. When the proper buttons were pushed on the instrument board and the destination was set on the automatic chart the controls of the space ship were locked. And they would not be unlocked until the space ship reached the indicated destination—in this case the Rocky Mountains.

"Willie," said Eddie, "Marty had to get out of that damp cloud. Earth moisture is bad for Martinean engines . . . makes them disinter . . . disinterate. I mean disintegrate . . . like maybe sort of fall apart or to pieces and lose power. Now that's a lot worse up here in the air than going to the Rocky Mountains, isn't it?"

Willie nodded.

"But we come right back. You hear," he admonished Marty.

Marty nodded cheerfully and then he shouted, "Hold breath for landing."

ZO-OM! The space ship plunged earthward and came to rest as gently as dandelion fluff on the tiptop of the highest peak jutting out of the Rocky Mountain range.

"This United States Rocky Mountains," said Marty.

They looked out at the bleak mountain tops through the transparent bubble of the space ship.

"It sure is," said Willie. "Now let's go home."

"No exploration?" asked Marty. He looked at the timepiece on his wrist and added, "From New York to United States Rocky Mountains two minutes, eleven seconds."

"Boy, that sure is good time," said Eddie. He looked at his watch too. "Say, it's only half-past four. You don't eat supper until six o'clock, do you, Willie?"

"That's right," said Willie. "But Amsterdam Avenue is pretty far away."

"We could do just a little exploring, couldn't we?" said Eddie. "It'd take only a few minutes to get to New York. You could be home long before six. We could explore just a little . . ."

They all looked out at the dismal mountaintops and down the sharp rocks to the wilderness below.

"Explore where?" asked Willie.

After a few minutes they all decided they'd go and explore someplace else on another day . . . tomorrow.

The space ship blasted off again and in three minutes flat they were again back in the wooded dell in back of the old brick lion house in the New York zoo.

"There," said Eddie, "I told you it wouldn't take long, Willie. Now you have plenty of time before supper."

And after deciding to meet tomorrow to do some real exploring (even Willie was enthusiastic now that they were safely home) Eddie and Willie trotted back to Amsterdam Avenue. Marty would stay in his tent, which he put up under a bush in the wooded dell where he hid his ice-cream-cart space ship.

3. The Interplanetary Explorers

RIGHT after breakfast the next morning Eddie and Willie ran over to Central Park Zoo. They were both wearing their Boy Scout shirts (with the merit badges on them) just in case Marty decided to do some real exploring again.

"Eddie," said Willie as they jogged along the street, "that Marty man sure knows his thing. The way he pops his little space ship right up into the air and goes shooting off to the Rocky Mountains and right back again . . . right on the button, a pinpoint landing. What a man!"

"Yep," said Eddie, "he sure is."

Of course Eddie knew that Marty could make a pinpoint landing now that he had learned how to handle his space ships. He had some trouble with the first two space ships he had used in his first two visits to Earth. The first space ship was immobilized because Marty lost or mislaid the Secret Power Z that propelled his ship.

And he had trouble with his second space ship (which was a very modern ship) because he had not learned to fly it properly up on Martinea before he blasted off to Earth. While exploring the United States he missed his planned destinations by a number of thousand miles again and again. He landed in Florida when he aimed at Washington, D.C. and by-passed Washington again going north to the Arctic Circle.

He called these trips "small mistakes." But he carefully studied his handbook on how to fly a space ship as he sat around Eddie's grandmother's barn. And before his return to Martinea he was able to pinpoint his landing.

Eddie and Willie jogged along silently, each of them with his own thoughts. They got to the wooded dell behind the old brick lion house in the zoo without much conversation.

They found Marty tinkering with his ice-cream-cart space ship. Neither Eddie nor Willie was wearing visualizers so they did not see the space ship; all they saw was Marty ducking head-first into the ice-cream cart. But they knew he was really working on the space ship. As soon as they put their visualizers on they could see it. Marty had

taken some parts out of it and the parts rested on the grass and on the path.

"Hiya, Marty," said Eddie, and Willie said, "Hi."

Marty pulled his head and body out of the ice-cream cart. He was wearing his regular green Martinean Spaceman's uniform and his Boy Scout shirt on top of it. His nose was smudged.

"Hello, Scouts," he said cheerfully. "Ready to go explore?"

"You bet," said Willie with a grin. "Put that thingamumjig together again and let's go."

Marty looked around. "Where is thing-a-mum-jig?"

Eddie spoke up hastily, "Willie means the space ship. He was making a joke like the man did yesterday."

"Joke? Joke?" repeated Marty. "This means not truth, you said . . ."

"Oh, Marty," interrupted Eddie to change the subject, because he believed Marty would never understand what a joke was, "where you going exploring? And say, why did you come to planet Earth this time anyhow?"

"Not explore planet Earth," said Marty. "Explore planet Xonia."

"Planet Xonia. Never heard of planet Xonia," said Willie, who had a merit badge in astronomy. "Where is this planet Xonia?"

"Planet Xonia on no-light side of Moon . . . 252,178 Earth miles," said Marty, as he pointed straight up to the sky.

"Oh . . . no-light side of Moon? What's that?" asked Willie.

"Guess Marty means on the dark side of the Moon," said Eddie, who had had experience with Marty's English. "You know, the side of the Moon that never faces the Earth."

"On the dark side of the Moon?" said Willie. "So what are you doing here on Earth, Marty? Why'd you come to this planet?"

"Earth good base for interplanetary explorers to explore planet Xonia," said Marty.

"What d'you mean by that?" asked Willie.

"Well, Marty knows what he's talking about," said Eddie. "He knows a lot."

"What'd he mean by interplanetary explorers? Where's the interplanetary explorers? Does he mean us?" asked Willie.

"Marty," asked Eddie, "d'you mean you want Willie and me to go exploring the planet Xonia with you? D'you mean that, Marty?"

Marty looked at Eddie with a surprised look on his face as if Eddie was the one who had suggested that he, Eddie,

and Willie would like to go exploring the planet Xonia on the dark side of the Moon. He smiled broadly and nodded his head vigorously.

"Well, I dunno," said Eddie.

"What's eating you, Eddie? It's a good idea," said Willie enthusiastically. After yesterday's trip to the Rocky Mountains and back Willie had complete confidence in Marty.

"How long do you figure it will take," asked Eddie, "to fly to planet Xonia and explore and return to Earth?"

Marty knit his brow and tried to figure it out with mental arithmetic. He gave that up and got out a small machine from one of his pockets. He pressed buttons and moved tiny levers on the little machine. It whirled, blinked lights, clicked, rang tiny bells, and then suddenly stopped. Obviously, it was a Martinean mathematical calculator.

Marty read the final results of the little machine's calculations. It appeared in Martinean numbers on the face of the machine.

"Journey to planet Xonia . . . time to explore . . . return to planet Earth . . . three-quarter Earth rotation around on axis . . ." And then he explained, "Three-quarter Earth-day."

"Three-quarter day!" exclaimed Willie. "That's eighteen hours. Let's see. It's eight o'clock in the morning now. Then eight at night. That makes it twelve hours. Then six hours more. We'd be getting home after midnight! No sir. My mother won't be letting me do that."

"Mine either," said Eddie.

Marty consulted his calculator again. He pushed other tiny buttons and moved other levers. And the little machine whirled, blinked lights, clicked, and rang more tiny bells. The result of the new calculations appeared on the face of the machine. After Marty studied them he consulted the instrument on his wrist that served him as a watch.

"Leave Earth 8:15 A.M. Return from planet Xonia 8:15 P.M." he announced triumphantly.

"Well, that's not bad . . . let's go," said Eddie. He looked at his own wristwatch with the compass on the back and yipped, "Say, it's five minutes after eight now. I gotta let my mother know I'll be late for supper."

"Me too," said Willie.

"We won't have time to run to Amsterdam Avenue and back in ten minutes," said Eddie. "Hey, Marty, where's that telephone you used when you called me yesterday from the zoo?"

"No call on telephone," said Marty.

"But, Marty, I talked to you on our telephone."

"Call on Interplanetary Communicator Diminutive," said Marty. "Transmit message to Martinea, reflect to Zurianomatichrome Wire in your house."

Eddie gulped.

"Oh, you mean the message went all the way to Martinea and then bounced back to Earth to my house to that Boy Scout badge you made out of Secret Power Z wire?" he asked in amazement.

Marty simply nodded.

A few summers ago Marty gave Eddie a going-away present. Marty twisted a Boy Scout badge out of a shiny piece of wire made of Zurianomatichrome—the Secret Power Z that propelled Marty's first space ship.

That was the time Eddie gave Marty a history book and an old Boy Scout *Manual.* Eddie kept that shiny, silver Boy Scout badge in a box with other treasures in a drawer in the telephone table at home. He had told Marty he did not wear it only because it was not a regulation Boy Scout badge.

"What'dya know about that?" said Willie, after Eddie quickly told him the story.

"Can I use that Interspacial Communicator thing or whatever you call it, Marty, to call my mother and tell her I'll be late for supper?" asked Eddie.

"Yes, can use," said Marty. He took out a shiny disk about the size of a silver half-dollar. He pressed the button on the rim and that one disk became two connected by a short rod. Marty turned up one of the disks at a right angle to the other.

He showed Eddie how to talk into it. One should talk

into the turned-up disk and put the other disk against his ear.

"Man, just like a crazy telephone," said Willie.

Marty shook his head and said, "No telephone."

He handed the communicator to Eddie and showed him the right button to press. Eddie warily put his ear to one disk as he held the other near his mouth. He pressed the button Marty had indicated, then he heard the same crackling, swishing, roaring sound he had heard when he answered Marty's telephone call at home.

At last he heard the sound of a ringing telephone and then his mother's voice.

"Hello . . . hello . . ." said his mother.

"Hello, Mom," shouted Eddie. "Listen, I'll be late . . ."

"Eddie, please don't shout," said his mother. "We have a very poor connection. We must get this phone fixed. I hear the strangest sounds on the phone, and then you shout . . ."

"Speak natural," whispered Marty into Eddie's ear.

"What was that?" asked Eddie's mother. "What did you say? Now you're talking too low."

"Mom," said Eddie, "Willie and my friend Marty . . . remember him? Grandma told you about him. Well, Willie and Marty and me are going to do a little exploring . . . I'll be late for supper."

"Oh," said his mother. "Oh, very well, not too late. I'll keep things warm for you . . . But Eddie, what about your lunch? Remember, you're a growing boy."

"I gotta quarter, Mom. I'll buy a hot dog or something."

"Get an all-beef hot dog, Eddie," said his mother. "It's more nutritious."

"Ask her to tell my mother about me too," hissed Willie into Eddie's ear, "I got lunch money too."

"What was that, Eddie?" asked his mother. "Now take care of yourself and—"

"Oh, Mom," interrupted Eddie, "tell Mrs. Jackson Willie's going exploring too . . . He's got lunch money."

"All right, Eddie," said his mother. "Have a good time. Remember, not too late. I'll go right next door and tell Mrs. Jackson about Willie. Good-bye, Eddie."

"Good-bye, Mom."

Eddie gave the Interplanetary Communicator back to Marty.

"Thanks, Marty," he said. "It worked great. Say, Marty, have you got any food or water on the space ship or the big astro rocket disk?"

"On Astro Rocket Space Ship have concentrated food, concentrated water," said Marty.

"Hmm," muttered Eddie, who had eaten concentrated food in Marty's space ship before. "D'ya mind if I take along a hot dog on a bun?"

"Dog hot?" said Marty. "No . . . no animals on satellite space ship."

"Oh, Marty, hot dog is not an animal. It's something to eat," said Eddie. He did become impatient with Marty's English sometimes.

"Eat dog hot?" said Marty, as he shrugged his shoulders and returned to work on the space ship. "Yes, bring dog hot."

"O.K. I'll run and get one," said Eddie.

"Get me one too," said Willie, digging some money out of his pocket. "Look, Marty, I got money enough for two.

Can I buy you a hot dog? It's awful good with lots of mustard and pickles and stuff on it."

Marty thought of his concentrated food. Then he nodded his head too.

"Yes, bring dog hot," he said.

"O.K.," said Eddie, after he took Willie's money, "I'll be back in a minute."

"Remember, I want the works on mine," shouted Willie after him.

By the time Eddie came back clutching three hot dogs dripping with mustard, sauerkraut, piccalilli, chili sauce, and a few dashes from a few other bottles on the hot dog cart, Marty and Willie had the space ship assembled and they sat in it waiting for him to come aboard.

After Eddie climbed on and Marty slammed the side door of the space ship shut, they sat there as Marty closely watched the instrument on his wrist that served him as a timepiece.

"Blast-off in three minutes to rendezvous with Astral Rocket Main Space Ship," he explained as he delayed the takeoff now that they had their hot dogs and were all ready to go.

Eddie told Willie that the large Astral Rocket Space Ship was orbiting the Earth right now and Marty was waiting with his satellite space ship until the right moment to blast off into space—just as the Astral Rocket Ship was exactly overhead (aboye Central Park) in its orbit around the Earth.

Willie nodded again and again as Eddie talked. He knew about such things. He'd read up on space ships and orbiting and things like that. And he did have an aviation merit badge. He explained some things to Eddie.

As they talked an old lady carrying a crumpled bag, half full of bread and cake crumbs, appeared at the end of the path.

"Did you see any pigeons looking for their breakfast around here?" she asked.

"No, ma'am," said Eddie.

"Why don't you boys sit on a bench instead of in an ice-cream cart?" she said. "There are lots of empty benches this time of morning. If you do see any pigeons . . ."

At that moment Marty pushed the blast-off button. And Z-O-O-M, the space ship satellite took off.

"They seemed in an awful hurry," muttered the old lady as she turned away to look for pigeons. "That's the trouble. Everybody is always in a hurry . . . If people took a little time and thought about our little feathered friends . . ." She went off shaking her head.

4. Klunko . . . Junko!

WITHIN one minute and ten seconds after blast-off the little satellite space-ship perambulator had reached the proper orbit and leveled off for a rendezvous with the big Astral Rocket Space Ship. Marty pushed the proper button to stop the satellite's ascent and they hovered in the stratosphere high over the Earth. Marty watched the time machine on his wrist very intently.

He muttered, "Ten . . . nine . . . eight . . . seven . . . six . . . five . . . four . . . three . . . two . . . one."

Then he turned anxiously every which way.

"Where Astral Rocket Space Ship?" he said with a worried frown.

Willie, who was looking back at that moment, shouted: "H-e-r-e she COMES!"

Just in time Marty pushed a button to send the satellite forward at the proper speed so that there would be no shock as the front of the speeding Astral Rocket Space Ship coupled properly with the little satellite. They coupled with hardly a tremor.

The boys felt a slight nudge as the little satellite docked smoothly into the hollow nose of the advancing Astral Rocket Space Ship.

"Marty, man! You sure know your space ships!" burst out Willie in admiration.

Marty was not exactly sure what he meant. But Willie was smiling when he said it so Marty smiled too.

"Now change course . . . direct to Moon," he said.

He pushed the necessary buttons and levers and then with a powerful blast of rocket power from the big Astral Rocket Space Ship, they broke out of the orbit around the Earth and headed for the Moon and the tiny planet Xonia.

Eddie and Willie never did see the interior of the large space ship. It was mainly full of rockets and concentrated fuel (Secret Power ZZZ plus one). There was very little room for anything else in it, Marty told them, except a storage of concentrated food and water.

All the actual activity, movement, and function in this type of big Martinean Astral Rocket Space Ship was usually controlled by smaller satellites such as Marty's perambulator. Of course, most of the Martinean satellites were a lot bigger than Marty's little space ship.

For a while Marty was too busy to explain any more about the mechanics of his space ship or anything else. He was busy steering the space ship past what he called "primitive Earthman contraptions."

He meant the various scientific satellites that were rocketed up into space by the United States and other countries on Earth in an effort to study atmospheric composition,

weather problems, and to solve scientific mysteries of space.

These various contraptions, which Marty called primitive, orbit the earth long after their equipment has stopped working and they crowd up the space around the world like a floating junkyard. Eddie had read that in a newspaper article once.

Again and again Marty swerved his space ship out of the path of some object with antennas and other curious structures sprouting out of it that whirled by. Each time Marty muttered something in his Martinean language that sounded like "Klunko."

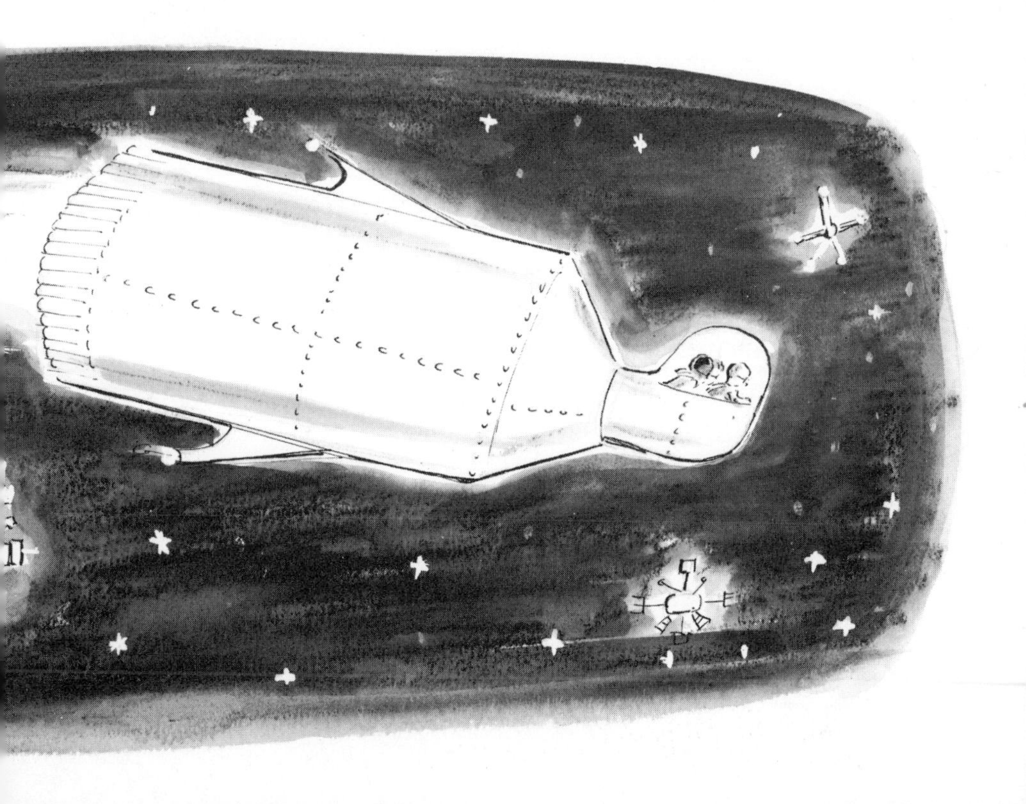

“What’s this ‘Klunko’ that you’re saying mean?” asked Willie.

Since there were no whirling Earth satellites in sight, Marty answered his question.

“Klunko means . . . no use material . . . waste material,” he said.

“You mean stuff that people throw away, stuff that’s no use to anybody, like junk? Does Klunko mean junk?” asked Eddie.

Marty thought a moment. Then he nodded.

"Hey, man, that's pretty good," cried Willie. "Klunko . . . junko . . ."

From then on until they cleared the area in outer space affected by the Earth's gravity, every time an Earth satellite came along the first one who saw it would shout out, "Klunko, junko," and Marty would steer away from it.

When they finally rocketed out to clear outer space Marty pushed the proper buttons on the instrument board, set the destination on the automatic chart, and leaned back with a sigh of relief.

"Now direct to Moon," he said.

He was ready to answer any questions the boys had been asking ever since the little space ship perambulator docked into the big interplanetary Spacial Astral Rocket Space Ship.

"Now answer questions," said Marty. "One question . . . one answer."

Willie and Eddie started talking at the same time.

"What time will we get to Xonia?" asked Eddie. "What's special about Xonia? Why do you wanna go there?" asked Willie. "Is it cold or warm in Xonia?" asked Eddie.

Marty put up his hands.

"One question . . . one answer," he repeated sternly.

"All right, go ahead, Willie," said Eddie. "You ask first."

"O.K. What's special about Xonia?" asked Willie. "Why d'you wanna explore Xonia?"

Marty thought a moment. He always mixed up the words "special" and "spacial."

He asked, "Why Xonia 'spacial'?"

"I said special," said Willie, "not 'spacial.' Why are you gonna explore Xonia, not some other planet?"

"Xonia is smallest inhabited planet in Universe," said Marty. "No Martinean scientist explore Xonia, no Martinean scientist explore Earth Moon. I first Martinean scientist explorer to go observe Xonia and inhabitants."

Although Eddie knew, because Marty had once confessed to him, that Marty was not a first-class Martinean Scientist Explorer—only a Junior Scientist Explorer—he didn't say anything. He just listened as Marty talked.

Willie did not say anything either, but he shook his head for a moment.

"O.K. That's all right. But if your scientists never explored Xonia," he said, "how come they know there are living beings on that planet?"

"Receive positive vibration from Xonia on Interplanetary Communicator . . . sound of living inhabitants," said Marty.

"That's like the U.S. scientists down in Texas, checking the heartbeats of our astronauts on the Moon," exclaimed Eddie.

Marty shrugged.

"But look, Marty," said Willie, "is that the only reason you're coming all the way from Martinea—to observe the inhabitants of Xonia? Seems like a pretty long trip just for that."

For a moment Marty was silent. He seemed to be making up his mind about something. He looked around the

little space ship and out into the black sky that surrounded them, as if he expected some dangerous strangers to be lurking in the darkness. Then he whispered, "Now tell complete truth like Boy Scout. Explore Xonia for possible source of important pure materials to make Zurianomatichrome . . . Secret Power Z!"

That disclosure astounded both boys.

"Secret Power Z!" gasped Eddie. "Material to make Secret Power Z!"

"Zowie! Man, that's something," exclaimed Willie.

"Keep voice down!" hissed Marty sternly.

"But Marty, how come the Martinean scientists figure there's pure materials for making Secret Power Z on a little planet millions of miles away from Martinea?" asked Eddie.

Marty said that Martinean scientists send out research beams all over the Universe to hunt for the materials to make Secret Power Z. Martinea was running short of its supply.

When the scientists had sent research beams to Xonia they had received definite response that indicated there were some pure materials in that little planet. Through their research beams they already knew that such essential pure materials were buried deep in the Moon.

Marty went on to explain that Martinean scientists believe that the Moon was part of the Earth millions of years ago, and it broke off and became an Earth satellite. They also believe that Xonia broke off the Moon and became a Moon satellite.

But even though the scientists know there is no life on the Moon they have a theory that the piece of the Moon that broke off millions of years ago and became Xonia

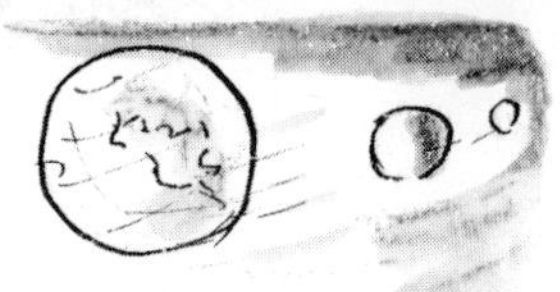

carried with it a few living cells that were the same cells that eventually developed into man and the other creatures of the Earth.

"This process of evolution," said Marty, to clarify things.

"Evolution!" exclaimed Willie. "That's it. I read about evolution in a book about Charles Darwin."

"Native of Xonia equal Earthman," said Marty.

"How come natives of Xonia and natives of Earth—Earthmen, I mean—and natives of Martinea—you, Marty—are all the same?" asked Eddie.

"Same? Same?" repeated Marty, his brow wrinkled. "What means same?"

Sometimes Marty forgot English words he had learned. Eddie was sure Marty knew the word "same."

"Oh, you know, Marty. I mean they are all sort of equal," said Eddie.

"Not same . . . not equal," said Marty. "Native of Xonia, Earthman, native of Martinea no same, no equal . . . Martinean much more superior . . . more advanced. Earthman more primitive. Native Xonia equal primitive."

"I mean we all have two legs, two arms, two eyes, and one head, and things like that," said Eddie. It sounded as if he were apologizing for saying Earth people are equal to the scientifically advanced Martineans.

"All people are equal," said Willie firmly.

"Yes, this way equal," said Marty. "This best design for superior creature live in equal atmospheric environment."

"Environment? What's that?" asked Eddie.

"You know, Eddie," said Willie. "I read about that too. It means . . . like saying living conditions. We all breathe air . . . you know oxygen . . . and live in the same climate and stuff like that."

Marty nodded. "Yes, this means environment."

"Oh," said Eddie slowly, and he tucked that new word "environment" away in his memory.

"Marty, how long will it take to get to Xonia?" asked Eddie. "I mean, what time will we get there?"

Marty thought a moment. Then he figured it out on his computer.

"Arrive Xonia 12:30 P.M. United States eastern standard time," he said. "Velocity 123,671 Earth miles, one Earth hour."

"Only 123,671 miles an hour! Is that all?" exclaimed Willie. "Eddie, I thought you said Marty travels almost about as fast as the speed of light."

"This low velocity necessary," explained Marty apologetically. "Must arrive Xonia beginning daylight time when sun on other side of Moon . . . when Xonia daytime begin."

"What time does daytime begin on Xonia? How long is a day on Xonia?" asked Willie.

"Daylight time begin now 12 P.M. United States eastern standard time. Arrive Xonia after long night. Xonian inhabitants awake after long sleep."

"How long is a day on Xonia?" asked Willie.

"Xonia daylight time fourteen Earth revolutions around sun . . . fourteen Earth days," said Marty. "Nighttime fourteen Earth days. Xonian sleep fourteen nighttime Earth days."

"Man, oh man, fourteen days of darkness," said Willie, shaking his head.

"How come their days and nights are so long?" asked Eddie.

Marty pointed to a map over his instrument panel. It was a finely drawn, astronomical map of that part of the Universe that includes all the planets and all the satellites which orbit around them in our sun's solar system.

He pointed to a tiny circle that was the Earth. And then to an even tinier circle that was the Earth's Moon. And at last to a pinpoint close to the Moon that was the planet of Xonia. He explained that the Moon does not rotate like the Earth. And that the Earth people always see the same face of the Moon.

When the Moon in its orbit is closer to the sun, the dark side of the Moon faces the sun. And when the Moon revolves to the other side of the Earth it is lit up by the sun and the people on the Earth see the lit-up Moon at night. Xonia has the same light and dark periods as the Moon.

Eddie found Marty's explanation hard to understand. But Willie nodded his head again and again as Marty talked. He understood about those things, since he had a merit badge in astronomy and had read up on the subject. He took a small paper book about astronomy out of his pocket. There was a map in the book that showed a diagram of the Moon, the Earth, and the sun. The diagram showed how the Moon was lit up by the sun and became full and then how it waned and became dark every month.

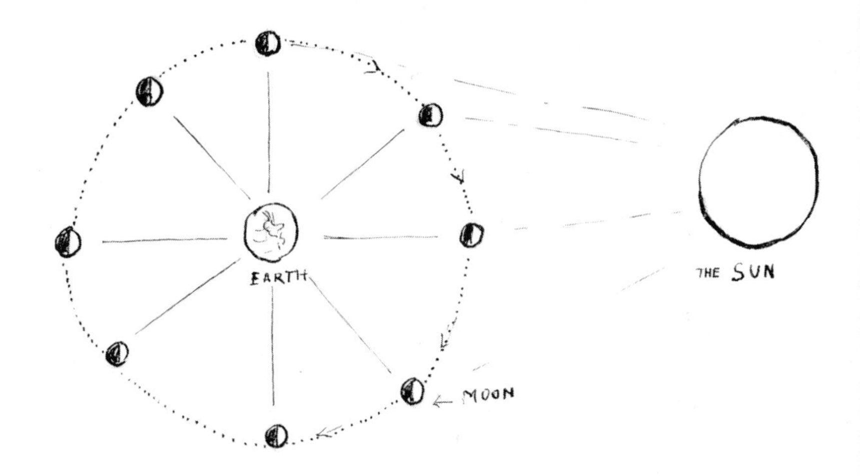

At last Eddie thought he understood and he nodded his head.

"Yeh," he said slowly, "I guess that's so."

After Marty answered a few more questions he suggested they eat their lunch—the hot dogs he had tucked away in a small locker under his instrument board. He said he expected to be very busy when the space ship reached the Moon's gravity belt. He would have to maneuver the space ship carefully past the Moon because he knew there were primitive Earth contraptions circling the Moon too.

The hot dogs were cold by this time but they all enjoyed their lunch. Marty did not like mustard. He tried to scrape the mustard off his hot dog with one of his little machines and he almost lost the whole hot dog into the nozzle of the machine.

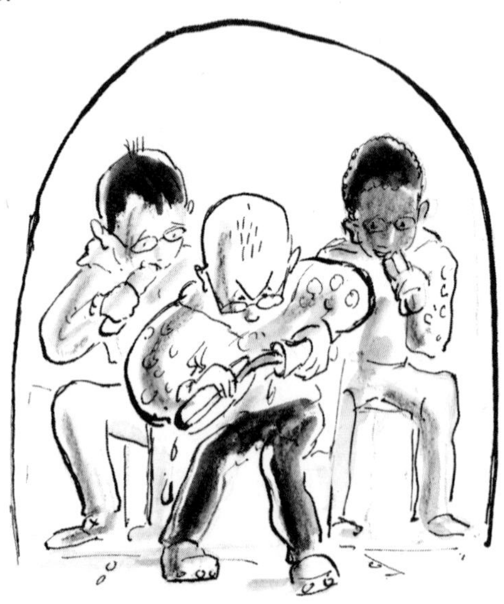

As they were eating their hot dogs Eddie asked, "Hey, Marty, how come we got no trouble eating and swallowing these hot dogs here in outer space like this?"

"Yeh, how come?" asked Willie. "I read about the Earth's astronauts floating around in their space ships and having trouble with food because there's no gravity or something like that."

After Marty understood their questions he lifted his eyebrows and shrugged his shoulders.

"Earth astronauts in very primitive space ships," he said with what seemed like a slight sneer. "Martinean scientists adjust environment in Martinean space ships equal to normal atmospheric pressure, normal gravity, normal conditions on planet Martinea. Equal . . . same planet Earth."

The Moon was just beginning to wane as they rocketed into its gravity belts. The gravity pull toward the Moon was not very strong. But it did affect the course of the space ship. And Marty was on the alert again for Klunko, as they called the Earth's man-made contrivances that orbited around the Moon.

He had adjusted the automatic chart so that he could steer the space ship manually in case of just such an emergency as he faced now.

Willie and Eddie were also intently watching out for Klunko and would shout out, "Klunko, junko," when they spotted any.

Suddenly Marty called out:

"Now orbit Moon."

The space ship whirled around the silvery gray shape of the Moon. They orbited the Moon once from the sunlit side of its surface around to the dark side and out into the light again.

"Say, Marty," said Eddie, "can we get closer to the Moon to get a real good look at it?"

Marty nodded and steered the space ship into a lower orbit.

At the lower orbit the boys could clearly see the huge craters and crevices on the surface of the Moon. As the space ship whirled low over the lighted surface of the

Moon they saw signs of the recent visit by the United States astronauts.

Marty pointed them out.

A United States flag hung limply on a pole in the still atmosphere of the Moon. And there were a few curiously shaped machines scattered about.

"Look at the way that flag hangs," said Willie. "They should have put an electric fan there to keep that flag flying."

Marty also pointed out some other man-made machines.

"Somebody else must have sent some stuff up to the Moon too," said Eddie.

"Sure they did," said Willie, "but only the United States sent astronauts who landed on the Moon."

The space ship had reached the outer rim of the sunlit portion of the Moon and was whirling around into the darkness on the other side.

"Look," said Marty sharply. He was pointing to a spidery tower with green lights blinking on it that they could hardly see in the dim twilight between the dark side and the sun-lit side of the Moon.

"This Martinean Scientific Station," said Marty proudly. This station erected by Martinean scientists five hundred Earth years past . . . continuous perfect performance!"

"Man, oh man . . . That's some tower!" said Willie. "But listen here, Marty, you said the Martinean scientists never explored the Moon. How come they built a big tower like that if they never landed on the Moon?"

"Martinean Scientist Explorers never explore Moon," said Marty. "This Martinean Scientific Station erected by remote control from Martinea."

"Remote control!" exclaimed Willie. "Man, that's crazy! That's impossible! Nobody could build a tower like that that way."

"No, Willie, it's not impossible," interrupted Eddie. "Remember how the machines and stuff sent to the Moon are controlled by the U.S. scientists down in Texas. Now I saw things on Martinea . . ."

And Eddie told Willie about the space ships, machines that make machines, even baby carriages and lots of other things that he saw controlled by remote control on Martinea.

Willie just blinked, nodded his head, and did not say another word.

5. Cyfarchiad Dieidhryn

AFTER the second orbit around to the dark side of the Moon Marty again changed the course of the space ship and steered directly to the planet Xonia.

They hovered over the planet just long enough to release the little satellite space-ship perambulator from the big Astral Rocket Space Ship and then descended quickly to Xonia. The Astral Rocket Space Ship remained in space orbiting the planet.

The perambulator landed with a gentle jar on a small hill. Before they climbed out of the perambulator Marty reached into one of his pockets and brought out two rings. There was a shiny disk about as big as a dime attached

to each of them. He very solemnly gave one ring to Willie and the other to Eddie.

"This for defense if Xonia native declare war," he said. "Put on finger."

Marty showed them that he was wearing a similar ring on the middle finger on his right hand. The disk was turned in toward his palm.

"Now what's a little ring like that gonna do in a war?" asked Willie.

"This supersonic sonambulator . . . sends control ray. Stop advancing enemy," said Marty. "This sleep machine. Perfect defense weapon."

The boys put on their rings and Marty showed how they were to be used in case of attack. He thrust out his hand, palm open.

Then Marty opened the side door of the perambulator and they climbed out. In the dim light they could see very little of the surrounding territory.

"Now see planet Xonia," said Marty with a wave of his hand.

"There's not much to see," said Eddie, as he looked around at the barren landscape.

"We came a long way from Amsterdam Avenue to see nothing," said Willie, shaking his head slowly.

"No observe good," said Marty impatiently. "See Xonia City."

He was pointing to the hardly perceptible horizon. The boys squinted hard in the direction his finger pointed.

"What you talking about, man?" said Willie. "There's nothing . . . wait, yeh, I see it!"

"I do too," said Eddie.

In that gloomy light they both saw a few towerlike shapes jutting out of the wavering horizon.

Marty climbed back into the perambulator and the boys followed him. When they all were seated and the side door was shut Marty adjusted a lever and the little perambulator ran down the hill and scurried across the plain toward the city on the horizon at a good clip.

In a very short time they arrived in the strange city of Xonia.

The city seemed to have been built on a series of hills. There were no streets. Stairs went up and down the hills to the simple blocklike buildings. Some of the stairs were narrow with very small steps . . . others were wide with normal-size steps. And there were still others with very high steps.

These strange differences were true of the doorways of the block-shaped buildings. Some doorways were low and narrow, others were normal height but very wide, and there were still others that were very high.

In fact, those differences were true everywhere they looked. Stone benches and water drinking fountains were very low or high and the seats of the benches were very narrow or very wide. Some others could only be sat on by very tall people.

There was no sign of any of the inhabitants of Xonia City.

"This place is whacky," said Eddie.

"Yeh, crazy, man, crazy," said Willie. "Look at those crazy steps and that . . ."

As Willie was speaking they heard a door in one of the buildings being opened.

"Prepare defense," hissed Marty, and he thrust his arm out ready to open his palm.

Willie and Eddie put their arms out, too, ready to open their palms and throw the controlling ray of the supersonic sonambulator toward the Xonian native or natives in case there was any danger of attack. As they stood there taut and apprehensive one of the Xonian natives came out of the building.

He was a little brown man with a crown of white hair. He was wearing a long robe made of some coarse woven fiber. He came out rubbing his eyes and stretching as if he had just awakened. While he stood there yawning Marty called out to him.

The little man stopped in the middle of a yawn, stared at Marty and the boys, and dashed back into the doorway.

"What was that?" asked Eddie in a low voice." What did you say to him, Marty?"

"I say 'hello' in Martinean language," said Marty.

"Now how's that little man going to know Martinean?" asked Willie.

"Martinean scientist report Xonians speak language like Martinean language," said Marty. "Scientist hear Xonian speak on Interplan . . ."

Before Marty could complete his answer, the little man peered timidly out of the doorway again.

"Cyfarchiad Dieidhryn," he said gently.

Marty was bewildered.

"This language not Martinean," he said to Eddie out of the side of his mouth.

"Oh . . . you speak English," said the little man, and he came all the way out of the doorway. "Methought I heard you speak Welsh. I said 'Greeting, Strangers' in the language of ancient Wales."

"We all speak English," said Eddie.

Then the old man did something very strange. He bowed a deep graceful bow. It was almost a curtsy.

"Permit me to introduce myself," he said. "My name is Jones. Thomas Jones."

Marty bowed low and he said:

"Me Marty . . . here Eddie . . . here Willie."

Eddie and Willie tried to bow gracefully and curtsy the way the old man had done.

"Are ye Earthlings?" asked the old man.

"I Martinean," said Marty. He gestured toward Eddie and Willie. "Here Earthlings."

"Xonia is honored with your presence," said the old

man as he bowed again. "My forefathers were Earthlings. My great-great-great-great-great-grandfather came from the land called Wales on the planet Earth."

"Your great-great-great-grandfather was a Welshman?" exclaimed Eddie. "From the planet Earth?"

"My great-great-great-*great-great*-grandfather," corrected the old man.

"How'd he get here," asked Willie, "before there were rocket ships or things like that?"

"Ah, therein lies a tale," said the old man as he slowly nodded his head. "It is written in our scrolls of Xonia's history that an Earthling named Thomas Jones and his beloved wife dropped from the darkened skies onto our small planet three thousand long nights and three thousand long days ago . . . Hold, I shall show you the ancient scroll."

The old man ducked back into his house and while he was gone Marty pulled his little calculator out of his pocket. He pushed the proper buttons and moved the proper levers and the little machine whirled, blinked lights, clicked, and rang tiny bells. Marty studied the results and announced:

"Three thousand long nights, three thousand long days equal 229 and $\frac{9}{10}$ Earth years. Thomas Jones land on Xonia 229 and $\frac{9}{10}$ Earth years past."

By that time the old Xonian came out of his house again with a tattered scroll under his arm.

"This scroll . . . tells of Thomas Jones's memorable journey from Wales to Xonia," he said.

He unrolled the scroll and held it up for Marty, Willie, and Eddie to see. It was written in English but there were so many whirligigs and fancy twirls to the letters none of them could read it.

"What's it say?" asked Eddie.

"Are ye not well schooled?" asked the old man with a gentle smile. "This scroll is written in the purest English. But it is not necessary to read it. I remember every detail of the first Thomas Jones's journey written by that remarkable man himself."

And the old man went on to tell them of that famous trip—which may well be the first recorded flight of man into outer space—the journey of his forefather Thomas Jones and his wife from the little country of Wales on planet Earth to the smallest inhabited planet in the Universe, Xonia.

The first Thomas Jones was a brilliant young man who lived in Ungalineaw, a little village on the rocky coast of Wales on the planet Earth. He was an excellent shipbuilder, a very talented gunsmith, and an accomplished chemist.

In those days ships sailed the seas pushed by the wind in their sails, or rowed over the waves by the brawny arms of sailors. Thomas Jones dreamed of the time when ships would speed across the sea propelled by some other power, perhaps by the explosion of gunpowder. He built some small ships that were propelled by exploding gunpower . . . and then he thought of the idea of shooting a ship up into the skies.

At that time there were men who built large balloons which they hoped would carry them to the Moon. Of course, they all failed.

Thomas Jones built a tight ship on top of one of the bleak mountains of Wales. He built two large metal-encased gunpowder kegs at the base of the ship. He planned to explode a great quantity of gunpowder that would blast his ship into space. He did not expect to reach the Moon . . . but he hoped to rise above the clouds. As a precaution he rigged a large sail on the top of his ship. That, he hoped, would catch the wind and ease the fall of his ship as it returned to Earth.

When all was ready Thomas's young wife insisted that she would not permit him to blast off in his ship alone. She said that a wife's place is at her husband's side, come what may, come fair weather or foul. And Thomas had to make room for her on his ship. The interior of the ship was crowded with kegs of water, slabs of dried meat, and other provisions. It was evident to Mrs. Jones as she sat in Thomas's ship that he had expected to go far beyond the clouds.

Since Thomas Jones was a brilliant young chemist as well as a gunsmith and builder of ships he knew even in those ancient times that creatures who lived on the Earth

must have oxygen to survive. So he also stored a few kegs of concentrated solidified oxygen (prepared by a process he had developed) aboard his tight ship.

He secretly hoped that his ship would be blasted up into space by the explosion of his own gunpowder. And that it would rise far above the Earth and reach the area in the atmosphere where air becomes very thin and oxygen rare. Thomas Jones had often climbed high mountains up into the thin air on the mountain top. He always carried his prepared concentrated oxygen on those climbs.

At last Thomas Jones struck his flint against steel to spark the fuse that would explode the gunpowder in one of the great kegs at the base of his ship. And then . . .

B-O-O-M!

There was a thunderous explosion that sent the ship hurtling into space at tremendous speed . . . *and young Thomas had not yet fired his gunpowder!*

As he looked down at the fast-disappearing surface of the Earth he realized what had happened. Thomas had built his ship with its powder kegs on the very tiptop of an old volcano that had been inactive for hundreds of years. And just as he was preparing to send his ship up into the skies with the blast of gunpowder that old volcano had erupted!

It blasted its top off and threw Thomas's ship into outer space!

Thomas Jones found himself and his good wife in his tight ship orbiting the Earth in a very few minutes. Now he reasoned something must be done or he and his dear young wife and his good tight ship would continually orbit the Earth forever. Thomas Jones dared not think of that.

He decided now was the time to fire one of the great kegs of gunpowder at the base of the ship to try and blast out of the circling orbit and return to Earth.

But that did not happen. He fired that keg of gunpowder and blasted out of orbit . . . but not back to the Earth's surface. He blasted his ship into outer space.

For a number of days they whirled toward the Moon. Fortunately, the ship held enough water and food to sustain them and their oxygen supply was adequate. When they reached the outer limits of the Moon's weak gravity belt Thomas found his ship in orbit again . . . this time around the Moon.

Now Thomas fired the second keg of gunpowder and blasted out of the Moon's orbit. He and his young wife and his good tight ship were thrown into the atmosphere of Xonia and they landed on that planet . . . to the astonishment of the simple, gentle inhabitants of Xonia.

The sail on the top of Thomas's ship opened as it should and caught the wind. They landed with not too bad a crash. Thomas just broke one arm and Mrs. Jones sprained her ankle (it was very painful), and she suffered a few scratches on her nose.

Thomas Jones and his wife were well received by the gentle, peaceful, simple inhabitants and they lived happily forever after on the tiny planet of Xonia. They had many children and grandchildren who married the Xonians. That was why so many Xonians were named Jones, and why there were many young Xonians who had red hair on their heads. Mrs. Jones had very pretty auburn hair.

As the old Xonian talked, the other inhabitants quietly came out of their houses and stood in front of their doors or on the steps going up and down the hills. They were all dressed in long robes and many of the Xonians had bright red hair.

6. Magic Dust

"Now that you have patiently listened to our history," said the old Xonian, "What more can I tell you of our small planet . . . How can I serve you?"

"Why are the steps on the stairs all different sizes—high and low?" asked Willie. "And how come all the benches and the doorways and everything else are all different sizes?"

"The reason is lost in history," said the old Xonian. "They were always built that way—high steps for the tall, small steps for the small. All things were built that way in Xonia by the ancient Xonians."

"Where'd they get the stone to build with?" asked Eddie.

"Those stones were dragged to the hills from some distant area on the Xonian plains," said the old man.

Marty, who had been stealing glances at his timepiece as they listened to Xonian history, spoke up.

"What power in light?" he asked.

Marty pointed to the rows of lighted globes on poles that were placed on the side of the steps going up and down the hills. They lit the early Xonian morning with a cool blue light.

"They are lighted with our only power," said the old Xonian. "The source of the power is in the soil of Xonia."

Even as he talked a tall Xonian lifted some of the globes off the poles they rested on and put the globes in a bag. Those globes had lost their power and their lights were dim.

"The globes will be buried in a pit in one of our hills for a short time. Then their power will be renewed and they will glow with a bright light again," said the old Xonian.

"Where pit for bury globes?" asked Marty.

"All our hills have such pits. Here is one near my door," the old Xonian said, and he pointed to a slight depression in the ground at the side of his house.

Marty walked over to the little pit and stooped to pick up a pinch of the soil. He put the soil in a small vial he had taken out of his pocket. He shook it and then dropped a small black pellet into the vial and shook it again. Then he took the pellet out of the vial.

It glowed with a bright blue light!

"This very pure material for making Zurianomatichrome," Marty whispered out of the corner of his mouth to Eddie and Willie. "All hills with pure material to make Zurianomatichrome . . . must report to Martinea at once."

"Wait a minute," whispered Eddie.
"Are you sure, Marty?"

"Man, you ought to be sure," said Willie. "Can this stuff power space ships?"

The old Xonian had been talking to the tall man who was picking the dim globes off the poles.

He turned to Marty and the boys and said, "Command me . . . What are your desires? What can I tell you and what can I show you here on Xonia?"

"Where Xonian manufactories?" asked Marty.

"Manufactories?" repeated the Xonian. "I understand ye not. What are manufactories?"

"He means factories," said Eddie, remembering that manufactories was the word Marty used on Martinea when he meant factories. "You know . . . shops or buildings with machines that make a lot of things for a lot of people."

"Oh. We have none such," said the old man. "Our needs are few on this tiny planet. We all grow our own food. We weave and make our own robes. We build our own houses."

"What transportation on planet?" asked Marty. "Where make machines for swift transportation?"

"We have no machines for swift transportation," said the old man. "We have no reason for swift transportation on our small planet."

For a moment Marty was stumped. Willie asked some questions.

"Where are your stores? Where do you buy things?"

"Stores?" repeated the old Xonian gently. "We have no stores."

"Well, how do you get your food and things?"

"As I said, we all plant and raise the food we need," said the old man. "Let me show you."

He reached into a pocket of his robe and brought out some tiny seeds. With his finger he poked four small holes in the ground where they stood, and dropped a seed in each of the holes. Then he covered them over with a little soil. In a moment four plants began to grow. When they became about two feet high they flowered for an instant and then bore fruit.

The fruit of the plants was very much like tomatoes. The old man plucked four of them and gave one to each of the boys. After the fruit had been plucked all the plants withered and became dust again.

"Come join me at my first repast of the day," he said.

Marty, Willie, and Eddie nibbled gingerly on the large fruits. They did not taste at all like tomatoes. Willie, who had once eaten mango, said they tasted very much like a really good ripe mango with no seed in it. Eddie said they tasted like . . . a pineapple-orange-raspberry. Marty didn't say anything. He just grunted and ate the delicious fruit.

On all the hills the Xonians were either planting little

seeds in the soil or eating the fruits of the seeds they had planted. And they were not all eating tomatolike fruit. Most of the young Xonians were eating things that looked like curved bananas. The Xonian women were delicately eating pink grapelike fruits. They talked quietly and laughed gently as they ate.

"Do all Xonians get all their food this way?" asked Eddie. "Do you all grow your own food?"

"Why, yes . . . yes," said the old Xonian. He was surprised at Eddie's question. "Is there any other way?"

For a moment they silently watched some Xonian children on the hills playing a game like tag. On the steps that went up and down the hill others were playing a game that looked like hopscotch.

One of them tripped on the stairs and pushed another smaller Xonian child. The one who had tripped twisted his ankle and the small child who had been pushed tumbled down the stairs and bumped her head. A big lump swelled up on the little one's forehead.

But neither child cried out. They both quickly patted some of the soil from the hill on their wounds and were cured at once. They ran off to play again.

The old Xonian smiled and pointed to the children.

"All our bodily ills are made well again," he said, "with the magic powers in our soil. Aching heads, twisted or broken bones . . . the body pains that afflict the young, illnesses that afflict the old—all are cured at once by our soil."

"How do you get all the other things you need?" asked Willie.

"We have few needs. We grow this fiber that we weave for our robes just as we grow our food. The soil on our little planet has great power to actuate growth or to purify materials. We clean our robes and all our utensils, and we bathe in the dust. Here, behold the cleansing power of our soil."

The old man's fingers were stained a deep red from the juice of the fruit he ate for breakfast. He picked up some soil and rubbed it over his fingers. The deep red stain disappeared like magic. The boys did the same thing and rubbed the red stains from their fingers too.

"In the morning as we awake from our long sleep we roll in the dust in our bathrooms and begin the long day clean and refreshed," said the old Xonian. "Have ye all bathed this morning? Would any of ye bathe in our dust? There on that hill is one of our public bath pits. Our young Xonians would rather bathe and play in the magic dust of the public baths."

He pointed to a cloud of dust on the next hill. There were sounds of laughter and the voices of young people as they played and rolled in the dust pit.

Eddie and Willie had not had a bath that morning but neither one of them wanted a dust bath. Marty, Eddie knew, took his bath in certain beams of light. Eddie had bathed that way on Martinea too.

"Do you know what's in the ground here in Xonia that makes it so special?" asked Willie.

"No, we do not understand why or what is the power in the soil of Xonia," said the old man. "We do know that all we need—all the Xonians have ever needed—comes from the soil of our small planet."

Again Marty was fidgeting around and impatiently eyeing the timepiece on his wrist.

"Oh, forgive me," said the old Xonian. "Methinks I forgot all the manners my mother has taught me. You must need rest after your long voyage to our planet. Honor me with your presence in my humble abode. Wouldst repose for a while before you carry on your exploration?"

Marty nodded . . . to Eddie's and Willie's surprise.

The old Xonian opened the door of his little house and bowed as he indicated Marty and the boys should enter.

"When ye have rested well," the old Xonian said from the doorway, "I will be at your service once more," and he closed the door after him.

7. The Search

THE old Xonian's house was sparsely furnished. It was lighted by the same cool blue light that glowed from the globes on the poles along the hills.

"This Zurianomatichrome light," said Marty.

Eddie knew that. All of Marty's other space ships were lighted by the same cool blue light. There were no lamps in the old Xonian's house. The cool blue light glowed from the walls and ceiling of the little room.

There were two simple narrow benches along one wall and a few stools and a table along the other. They were made with the same fibers that were woven into the Xonian robes. Here the fibers were twisted and knotted together.

The bed, stool, and tables looked something like the old-fashioned wicker furniture Eddie's grandmother had in her parlor on the farm.

There were no windows in the room but it was airy and pleasant. Marty quickly looked around the room (even under the table and other furniture) as if he expected to see hidden microphones. And after he had completely and carefully inspected everything he whispered, "Now must contact Martinea."

Marty dug around in one of his pockets and got out his Interplanetary Communicator.

"Lookit, Marty," said Eddie. "Wait a minute, willya?"

"Yeh, man, can't you wait a minute?" said Willie. "What you gonna report to Martinea?"

"Must report pure material for making Zurianomatichrome in soil of Xonia," he said.

"But lookit, what's gonna happen when you report you found this pure material?" asked Eddie.

Marty knit his brow for a moment in deep thought and at last he said:

"Martinean scientists will develop process to transport pure materials to Martinea."

Marty began to press the proper buttons on his communicator to contact Martinea.

"But, man . . . what the Xonians gonna do if you take

their soil?" asked Willie. "How are they gonna get on?"

"Yeh, how?" asked Eddie. "You heard the old Xonian say the soil gives them everything."

Marty shook his head and looked away toward a corner of the room.

"Martinea needs Zurianomatichrome material," he said grimly. "This my duty. Must report presence of pure material."

"Lookit, Marty," said Eddie, "what you gonna tell the Martinean scientists? How much material is there?"

"That's it. Eddie's right," said Willie. "How much is there, do you figure? Is it all only in the hills or in the plains too? There was nothing on those plains we crossed when we came to Xonia City in your space ship."

Marty stopped fiddling with his communicator. Then he nodded.

"Yes, this true. Must find how much material in Xonia," said Marty.

"Yeh, man, you're right," said Willie. "And I think you oughta try to find out where it comes from. Where does that special power in the soil start?"

That did it. Marty folded up his Interplanetary Communicator and put it in his pocket.

"Must explore Xonia," he said. "Must test soil on plains for pure materials."

They quietly left the old Xonian's house, climbed aboard the space-ship perambulator that Marty had parked in back of the house, and went rolling down the hill to the

plains in a few seconds. The old Xonian was sitting on one of the stone benches talking to some children. He did not see them leave. The other Xonians they passed on the hill were surprised as the perambulator sped past them. They had never seen anything move so fast on their little planet.

Within a minute the perambulator was scurrying across the flat plain. When they reached the place where they had first landed on Xonia Marty turned a switch and the perambulator stopped. They climbed out and stood on the silvery-gray soil of the plains.

"Now measure pure material in plain," said Marty.

He took a roll of very thin wire out of one of his pockets and asked Willie to hold one end. Then Marty walked ten long paces away from Willie, unrolling the wire as he walked. Now he asked Eddie to hold onto the wire. Eddie did and Marty walked ten paces away from Eddie, still unrolling the wire. Then he pushed a small peg into the soil of the plain. He wound the wire around the peg, unrolled the wire, and walked ten paces back to Willie.

He asked Willie to hold the roll of wire as well as the end of it. Marty had made an equal-sided triangle with wire over the soil of the plain.

Now Marty went to the center of the triangle, scooped up a pinch of soil, and dropped it into the little vial with which he had tested the soil on the hill in Xonia City. Again he put a tiny black ball into the vial with the dust and shook it.

This time when he took the little black ball out of the vial it did not glow with the bright blue light the way it had when he tested the soil on the hill. Now the ball threw off a very dim light. Marty tested the soil in that triangle a number of times with the same result.

"No much pure material on surface of plain," he said at last. "Now test in depth."

Marty took a slender silvery-looking tube out of his pocket. He telescoped it out until it was about a foot long and he pushed the tube into the ground. Then he pressed a button at the end that stuck out of the ground. That end lighted up like a little fountain-pen flashlight. It was a red light.

After Marty had pushed the button to light up the tube he stood watching it very carefully. He seemed to be waiting for something to happen. He waited and he waited and he waited. Occasionally he would consult the timepiece on his wrist and shake his head . . . and he went on staring at the light and he waited some more.

"Hey, Marty, what's up?" asked Eddie. "Whatcha waiting for?"

"Yeh, man, how long am I gonna hold this little wire?" asked Willie. He was getting impatient.

Marty kept staring at the light. He held up one finger.

"This done soon," he said, and he waited another minute.

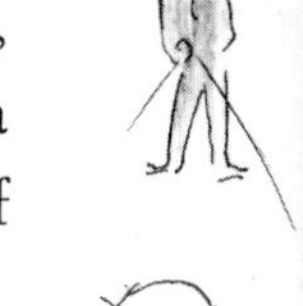

At last something happened. The little red light faded, became yellow, and faded again. And then it became a bright cool blue . . . and flashed on and off . . . on and off . . . on and off.

But Marty shook his head. He was disappointed.

"Now Telescopic Investigator Miniature reach exact center of planet Xonia . . . very small presence of pure material to make Zurianomatichrome in center planet Xonia," he said.

"How come . . . how do you know that?" asked Willie.

Marty explained that the little tube which he called the Telescopic Investigator Miniature had telescoped and drilled all the way down to the very center of the planet Xonia.

"You mean that skinny little tube went all the way down to the middle of the planet?" said Willie.

Marty nodded sadly.

"Are you sure, Marty?" asked Eddie.

Again Marty nodded and he stooped and touched a button on the little tube again. Now he waited, he said, for the extended part of the tube to come back to the surface.

"Must investigate more on plains," he said.

Marty pulled the little tube out of the ground, put it in his pocket, and rolled up the wire that Willie and Eddie had held. They all got back into the space-ship perambulator and scurried quickly across the plains. Marty stopped it again. He repeated his tests about a dozen times until it seemed he was convinced there was no pure material on the plains.

"Only place where find pure material to make Zurianomatichrome in hills in Xonia City," he said firmly. "Must test hills how much pure material."

They all climbed back into the perambulator and in a minute they were back in the city.

Marty made his tests very discreetly on the hills of the city. He only made them when he was sure none of the Xonians were watching him. He pretended he had dropped something, and then as he pretended to be looking for it he pushed the little Telescopic Investigator into the hill and covered its light with his hand as he crouched over.

He did his testing behind the houses on the hills. And after he had tested almost all of the hills of the city and found positive evidence that almost every hill was a mass of pure material for making Zurianomatichrome, he crouched over to make his last test. Then he heard a strange sound. He looked up quickly and found he was

looking directly into the bright blue eyes of a short dog.

The dog had been sniffing Marty's head!

It was a short dog, not a small dog. It had a normal-sized head, sharp nose, pointed ears, and long glowing silvery fur. But the dog had very short legs. He looked like a hammered-down silver-colored collie.

Right in back of the dog stood a little Xonian boy and a little girl who held another small short dog in her arms. Marty was surprised and he quickly flicked some soil over the light of his Telescopic Investigator.

"Hello," he said in English."

The little Xonian children said nothing. They just smiled.

Willie and Eddie, who had been watching Marty as they held the wire triangle around Marty's last test just the way they did for the other test, were just as surprised as Marty when they saw the little Xonians and the dogs.

"Hey, lookit, there's some dogs," cried Eddie. "Collie dogs. Where'd they come from?"

"Those are not collie dogs," said Willie. "They could be long-haired dachshunds. How'd they get here?"

"Step over wire. No see wire," Marty hissed to Willie. "Wire made of non-visual bamboozelurgical metal. Can be seen only with visualizers."

"Yeh. They came over the wire tied to the peg," said Eddie. He pointed to the tracks of the little Xonians in the dust.

"How'd you get dogs up here in Xonia?" Willie asked the Xonian children.

The little Xonians said nothing. They just smiled.

"I can answer that," said the old Xonian. He had just come around the corner of his house. It was there that Marty was making his last test. "The little Xonians know no English. Their mothers have only taught them to speak Welsh. They will soon be taught to speak English as a second language. Now then, these four-footed little creatures . . . the corgis . . ."

"D'you mean the dogs?" asked Eddie.

"Are they called dogs in the English language on the planet Earth? Here we use a Welsh word," said the old Xonian. "We call them corgis . . . The first Mrs. Thomas Jones brought two young corgis with her on the historic journey. She carried them in a pocket of her robe. These corgis are the descendants of those Welsh corgis. Every child on Xonia is given a little corgi as a companion. The children feed and care for these little creatures. Caring for and feeding the corgis, we find, develop many necessary virtues. It is part of the children's schooling."

As he talked one of the dogs barked. It was the strangest little bark either Willie or Eddie had ever heard. It sounded like the tinkling sound you sometimes hear from a silver cornet.

"What do they feed them?" asked Eddie. He didn't want to ask where the dogs got bones or canned dog food . . . that question did not seem right, somehow.

"Oh, the corgis are well fed," said the old Xonian.

The little corgi barked his little silvery bark again and the other corgi also barked a gentle little bark.

"Methinks they would be fed now," said the old Xonian. He turned and said something in Welsh to the little Xonians. They smiled and nodded.

Then the Xonian children took a few tiny seeds out of the pockets of their robes. They planted them and in a moment two plants grew, flowered, and bore fruit.

The fruits of the plant were the curved bananalike fruit that the young Xonians had eaten for breakfast. The little corgi crunched the fruit eagerly. The little curved bananas were hard and they crumbled like dog biscuits. The old Xonian said that the dry fruit was good for the young.

Marty managed to push the right buttons to retract his Telescopic Investigator. He pulled it out of the soil, rolled up the fine invisible wire that he had stretched to make his triangle . . . and slipped them into his pocket without anyone's seeing him do it.

The old Xonian told them more about the education of the young children on the planet. The young Xonians never

went to school. Their mothers went to school and they in turn taught their children the things they learned.

He said by that system if a mother had three or four or more children it was better to teach one rather than three or four. And the mother, the one who went to school, could teach her three or four children even when they had to stay home for a short time with sniffles or measles. (Yes, the little Xonians would get spotted up with measles occasionally, but they were not red spots. The little Xonians got green spots . . . and of course they were cured quickly with the soil from the hills.)

Then there were older Xonians who told the children

history stories and simple stories of astronomy. The old Xonian was one of the grown-ups who told them history stories.

"What about arithmetic?" asked Eddie. "Who teaches them fractions, decimals, addition, subtraction, and things like that?"

"Arithmetic?" repeated the old man. "Fractions, decimals, subtraction . . . what are these subjects? We do not teach nor do we know of these subjects."

"If you Xonians don't know arithmetic, adding, subtracting, decimals, and things like that," said Willie, "what do you do about money—when you pay for something, and get change for money?"

"Money? Money?" repeated the old Xonian. "We know nothing of money. We have no reason to pay anyone for anything."

Marty was anxious to get on with his testing. It seemed the silvery color of the dogs had given him an idea.

"All corgi equal color hair?" he asked.

"Equal color hair?" repeated the old Xonian. "Your meaning escapes me . . ."

"Marty means do they all have the same colored fur," said Eddie.

"Ah, yes. Their cloak of fur is always the same," said the old Xonian. "There's an old legend that has not been

recorded on any of our scrolls. It is said when the first corgis were brought to Xonia by Mrs. Jones the little creatures were a much darker hue, and with the passage of time they became lighter and lighter. Perhaps their fur is affected by their Xonian food."

"Where corgis sleep . . . where house?" Marty asked.

"All the little creatures live in caves on one hill," said the old Xonian. He pointed to a hill. "On that hill. The children who feed and care for them come and meet their little companions in the early morning and they bring them back to the corgi hill in the evening."

Now Marty could hardly wait. He was so anxious to begin testing the hill where the corgis lived he became almost rude. He frowned, looked at his timepiece, stood on one foot, then on the other, and at last he said:

"Must continue important exploration."

He ran to the perambulator and twitched his head as he passed Willie and Eddie to indicate he wanted them to come running too.

Eddie made some limp excuse to the old Xonian and he and Willie ran after Marty to board the perambulator.

8. Silver Noses

Marty did not steer the perambulator directly to the hill where the corgis lived. He sped down the nearest hills, whirled across the plains, and it was not until the City of Xonia was only a thin outline on the horizon that he changed his course.

He blasted the space-ship perambulator up into space and orbited once around Xonia, then descended in a flash to the hill where the corgis lived. After the perambulator landed he quickly explained that he had to disguise the place where he intended to do his important exploration from the old Xonian and the little Xonians.

No one was on the hill where the corgis lived. There were no Xonians and no corgis. Only two sets of stairs went up and down the hill. The stairs had low steps as if they were built only for little children. And there were no buildings on the hill.

One side of the corgi hill had a lot of little caves dug into it. And on the other side there were a number of small bathing pits dug into the soil.

Marty at once got to work again testing the hill. He had tested it before when he was testing the whole city of Xonia. This time he began another kind of test. He explained that since he was convinced this particular hill was very rich in pure material for making Zurianomatichrome, he was sure this hill was closest to the Secret Power that affected all the hills of Xonia.

"How did you figure out this hill is going to be closest to the Secret Power?" asked Willie.

"Hair on corgi dogs show sign of Zurianomatichrome,"

said Marty. "Source of power close to hill where corgis live."

Marty began to crawl into the caves where the corgis lived. He tested the walls and floor of all the caves. Willie and Eddie crouched down and watched him make his tests. He used the little black ball that he had used when he tested the soil. But he had another system. He held the little black ball in something that looked like a pair of silvery tweezers (the kind of tweezers Eddie's mother used to trim her eyebrows). And he would quickly rub the little black ball on the wall and on the floor of the little caves.

In all the caves the results were the same. The little black ball glowed brightly with a cool blue light every time. After the test in every cave Marty dipped the little black ball in a clear liquid in a transparent little vial.

The little black ball lost its bright cool light and became black again.

"What's Marty got in that little bottle?" Willie whispered to Eddie as they watched Marty make his tests. Marty heard his whisper.

"This Earth moisture," said Marty and he crawled into the next cave.

"What's Earth moisture got to do with it?" Willie asked Eddie.

"Marty told me Earth moisture—water, dew, soda pop, or anything like that—is not good for that Zurimata . . . whatever he calls it," said Eddie. "You know, the Secret Power Z. Earth moisture makes it lose power. That's why Marty dips the ball into Earth Moisture . . . water."

Marty, who had come out of the cave, heard Eddie's explanation and nodded. And then he crawled into the next little cave.

He backed out quickly from that one.

"Look!" he said. He was all excited as he pointed into the cave.

Willie and Eddie bumped heads together as they quickly looked.

There were three little baby puppy corgis all cuddled up sleeping on the floor of that cave!

And Eddie and Willie saw at once why Marty was excited. The little corgi puppies were not all silvery like the other corgis they had seen. These little corgis were almost all brown!

"What d'ya think of that? They must be just like the corgis that first came to Xonia," said Eddie.

"Yeah. They are pretty little brown dogs," said Willie.

Marty shook his head impatiently.

"No observe good. Most important sign of Zurianomatichrome . . . observe corgis' noses!" he said sharply, and he pointed into the cave again. "Look on noses!"

Eddie and Willie looked into the cave again and they saw why Marty was really all excited about the puppies.

Although the puppies were almost brown all over, their noses and faces were silvery and glowed with the cool blue light . . . the light of Secret Power Z!

Willie and Eddie pulled their heads out of the cave and sat down on the ground with their mouths open.

"Hey, man . . . how d'ya like that?" said Willie.

"How'd they get that way?" asked Eddie.

"From mother corgi dog," said Marty promptly. He was sure of it.

Then Willie and Eddie realized . . . that could be true. The puppies' noses and faces were silvery because like all babies they nuzzled their mothers.

Marty had his eyebrows all knotted up. He was thinking deeply. At last he made a decision . . . almost.

"Maybe . . . maybe source of Secret Power Z on Xonia come from old corgi dogs," he said slowly.

"From the corgis," exclaimed Willie. "Hey, man, that's crazy . . . that's impossible. Those little dogs can't be the source of the Secret Power Z."

"Sure, Marty, Willie's right," said Eddie. "The corgis may be close . . . closer than anything or anybody else to the source, but those little dogs can't be the source themselves. You can't be thinking of taking them all to Martinea."

Marty did not answer that. But he went on thinking, and he began to fiddle around in one of his pockets.

Eddie thought he was going to bring out the Interplanetary Communicator to contact the Martinean scientists. He was relieved when Marty took out another instrument from his pocket instead of the Communicator.

The instrument was silvery, like all of Marty's instruments. It was about as big as a ping-pong ball. Marty pulled a number of short antennas out of the little round instrument until it looked like a silvery pincushion. He crawled around the hill a number of times holding the little instrument near the ground and then he quickly went up and down the hill doing the same thing.

The instrument made a buzzing sound. And the tips of the little antennas blinked with tiny green lights. That's what happened when Marty tested the sides of the hill away from the corgi caves. But when he tested the side of the hill where the corgi caves were, the little instrument buzzed very loud. And the antennas no longer blinked green. They glowed with a steady brilliant cool blue light!

"Now very close to source of power," said Marty triumphantly as he stood up straight. He had been crawling so swiftly up and down and around the hill as he made his tests close to the ground that Eddie and Willie had to run to keep up with him.

But the little instrument did not buzz loudly or glow brilliantly when Marty stood up and lifted it away from the ground. Now it buzzed so loud it screeched, and the little antennas threw off brilliant blue sparks like a Fourth of July sparkler!

"Man, lookit that thing go," shouted Willie above the screech of the instrument.

"Will it explode?" shouted Eddie.

Marty shook his head. He too was surprised at the pe-

culiar behavior of his instrument. But he held it firmly and continued his tests. He lifted it slowly higher and higher until he held it up as high as he could reach over his head. The screech became shriller and the instrument threw off thousands of sparks, so that it looked as though Marty's whole hand had disappeared into them. Marty looked like a skinny little bald-headed Statue of Liberty as he stood there holding the sparkling instrument over his head.

"Source of power in atmosphere!" Marty shouted over the loud screeching sound.

"You can't take the whole atmosphere of Xonia up to Martinea . . . can you, Marty?" shouted Eddie.

Marty didn't hear him. He was looking up into the darkened sky over their heads. He looked up at the waning Moon.

Then Marty did something strange. As he faced the Moon he brought the little instrument down . . . and put it behind his back.

The screech of the instrument subsided and became a loud buzz again!

Then Marty brought the instrument around in front of him, and held it up over his head in the waning moonlight. Again the buzz became a loud screech . . . and again the glowing antennas became a mass of brilliant blue sparks.

Marty repeated that movement three or four times and he got the same results. When he exposed the instrument to the Moon it screeched and sparkled. When he held it behind his back and shielded it from the Moon the instrument just buzzed and glowed.

"Here source of power!" Marty announced as he pointed dramatically at the Moon.

“Where?” shouted Eddie.

“Y’mean the Moon, Marty?” shouted Willie.

Marty nodded.

“Yes . . . source of power from Moon,” he shouted.

“How d’ya . . . hey, Marty, will you shut that thing off?” shouted Eddie.

Marty turned around so that his body shielded the instrument from the Moon and as it buzzed he quickly pushed the little antennas back into the silvery ball . . . and the instrument was still.

“How you figure the source of power comes from the Moon?” asked Eddie in his regular voice. He was relieved that he did not have to shout anymore.

Marty shook his head.

"Must contact Martinea," he said. "Martinean scientists know answer to question."

Marty took his Interplanetary Communicator out of his pocket, contacted Martinea, reported to the scientists, and listened as they talked to him. At last he put the Communicator away. He evidently had the solution to the problem.

9. Source of the Secret Power

FROM somewhere in the little space-ship perambulator Marty got out some silvery rods with which he put together a tripod. And he topped it with something that looked like a very complicated surveyor's telescope.

He asked Willie and Eddie to each hold a length of the invisible fine wire as he peeked through his telescope directly at the Moon. Now and again he made notes in a book—the results of his observation through the telescope. Like a real surveyor Marty called out to Willie or to Eddie.

"Move this side four big steps . . . Move back one step . . . Stop . . . Now move three steps one-half forward."

Suddenly, as he was peeking through his telescope and calling out to Willie, he was surrounded by a flood of yap-

ping, barking corgis and laughing Xonian children! They came pouring over the side of the hill like a great wave!

Marty was swept off his feet by the onrush. His tripod was tumbled and his instruments were thrown out of his pockets and dumped all over the ground. The little corgis became entangled in the invisible wires that Willie and Eddie held. The children tried to untangle the little corgis and they too became entangled!

Marty became the unwilling center of a whirling, twisting, wiggling mass of yapping dogs and laughing children. Eddie, who was just at the edge of the wiggling mass, could see Marty trying to disengage himself from the heap of little dogs and happy Xonian children and Martinean instruments. He looked very angry! Suddenly out of the top of the swirling mass an arm and hand appeared! It was Marty's hand stuck straight up! It was the

hand on which he wore the supersonic sonambulator . . . the perfect defense weapon. Marty's hand turned this way and that, throwing the rays of his sleep machine all around him on the pile of dogs and children. In a moment they were still! They were all sleeping peacefully and snoring gently!

He easily picked his way out of the middle of the snoring group and quickly reclaimed the invisible wire that was twisted through and around the sleeping pile.

In another moment the dogs and children were all

awake again. The little Xonians hustled about, grabbing and chasing their own corgis, and in a little while order was restored. Many of the children said something in Welsh that sounded like an apology. They were all polite children.

And after things had quieted down one of the older children who evidently had been taught English by his mother stepped forward and said:

"Corgi go . . . bathpits . . . thank you." Obviously he did not know English too well.

Then the children, holding their corgis, ran over to the other side of the hill. Marty, Willie, and Eddie were alone again.

Marty picked up his spilled instruments, dismantled his tripod, and started to roll up the invisible wire.

"Are you quitting, Marty?" asked Willie. "Aren't you gonna test anymore?"

"You're not mad, are you, Marty?" asked Eddie anxiously. "Aren't you gonna finish . . ."

"Yes, finish," said Marty. "Now have absolute proof . . . source of power from Moon."

And he went on to explain that he had established by his last test that one of the beams carrying Secret Power Z from the Martinean tower on the Moon to the planet Martinea just grazed the top of the corgi hill as it passed the planet Xonia. That was why the corgi hill was the source of Secret Power Z that supplied all Xonia.

"Now must change direction of beam," said Marty.

"Are you sure you have to do that, Marty?" asked Eddie.

"Yes, this necessary," said Marty, and he dug into his pocket again for one of his instruments.

"How you gonna do it?" asked Willie.

"Will contact Martinea," said Marty. "Martinean scientists control Moon power by remote control. Scientists will change direction of Moon tower beam by remote control."

He took his Interplanetary Communicator out of his pocket, consulted his notes again, and began to press the buttons on his Communicator that would contact Martinea.

As he stood there waiting for Martinea to answer his signal some little Xonian children came around the hill with their corgis. They stood off at a distance politely and looked on. They all looked bright and clean and fresh from their dust baths. The little corgis' silvery coats of fur glowed with a cool blue light.

Marty was having some trouble getting his connection through to Martinea. He looked at the little children and dogs as they stood there quietly.

“Lookit, Marty,” said Willie, “can I ask you something?”

Marty nodded.

“Lookit, Marty, what’s gonna happen to the soil when the Martinean scientists change the direction of the beam from the Moon tower?”

Marty frowned and thought a moment.

“Soil on surface of Xonia become like surface on Moon,” he said. “Surface on Moon no life . . . no thing grow in Moon soil.”

“Man, d’ya mean these little kids won’t be able to grow their own breakfasts?” exclaimed Willie. He was horrified. “And the corgis won’t get their dog-biscuit fruit?”

Marty did not answer Willie. His Interplanetary Com-

municator made a beep-beep sound. He was in contact with the Martinean scientists.

He said a few Martinean words into the speaker of his Communicator. Then he listened as a distant scientist spoke to him. Marty looked at the notes he had scribbled as he peeked through his telescope at the Moon. He read his report into the Communicator speaker. And the scientist must have told him to stand by while they figured out a solution.

As he waited Marty looked off into the corner of the dark sky. He did not look at the clean little children or their pretty little corgis. And he carefully avoided the accusing eyes of Willie and Eddie.

Suddenly two of the little corgis popped out of the arms of two Xonian children. The dogs ran barking and yapping and chasing each other around and around in a circle. And then they dashed over to where Marty stood, with the Xonian children in swift pursuit. The dogs whirled around Marty, then through his legs, and then around and around again.

Marty frowned as he tried to keep from being tumbled again by the action of the happy corgis. He twisted around on his own legs and sat down hard on the ground. He

stood up again and looked angrily at the children and dogs.

The Xonians finally caught their dogs and after they mumbled some words that might have been an apology returned to the line of silent children and corgis.

The scientists from Martinea were talking again on the Communicator. Marty listened and answered some questions. And then it seemed he was arguing for something. Again he listened and again he talked—just two words—and that ended the conversation with Martinea.

As he carefully folded up his Interplanetary Communicator and put it away in his pocket he looked sternly at the line of gentle Xonian children and silvery corgis.

"What did they say on Martinea?" asked Eddie.

"What they gonna do? When they gonna begin?" asked Willie.

Marty held up his hand to silence them. He looked at the timepiece on his wrist.

"Now exploration of Xonia finish," he announced. "Must blast off for planet Earth . . . three minutes planet Earth time."

"But Marty, what's gonna happen here on Xonia?" asked Eddie. "Are you mad because the dogs made you fall down?"

Marty did not answer. He was already running toward

his parked space-ship perambulator. Eddie and Willie raced after him. They all climbed aboard the perambulator and Marty slammed the door shut.

He began to push buttons and wiggle levers on his instrument panel.

"Prepare for blast-off," he said. "Must rendezvous with Astro Rocket Space Ship."

"Marty, you're not gonna blast off from here, are you?" asked Eddie.

Marty turned and looked at Eddie. His eyebrows were high on his forehead.

"Why no blast off here?" he asked.

"You can't blast off without saying good-bye to the old Xonian," said Eddie, "now can you?"

"Yes . . . will say good-bye to old Xonian native," he said.

He rearranged the levers on his instrument panel and was about to push the button that would send the perambulator racing across the hills to the old Xonian's house. Now Willie had to ask the question that had been bothering him and Eddie.

"Marty, what's gonna happen about the Moon beam that gives Xonia Secret Power Z?" he asked. "When are the scientists gonna change the direction of the Moon beam?"

Marty silently fussed a little more with the levers on his instrument panel. His mouth was a thin line.

"No change direction of Moon beam," he said at last.

"Yeh, man, that's great," exclaimed Willie.

"Marty, you're a good scout," said Eddie enthusiastically.

Marty did not say anything. He just grunted and pushed the starting button.

10. The Message on the Moon

ZIP . . . ZOOM . . . BANG!

Marty zipped the perambulator across the hills to say good-bye to the old Xonian, zoomed the little spaceship up into outer space, and docked it with a slight bang to the nose of the big Astral Rocket Space Ship, which had been orbiting the planet Xonia—all that within a few minutes.

The space-ship perambulator was just a little too late for a smooth rendezvous with the big Astral Rocket Space Ship. That's why there was a definite banging jar as the little perambulator coupled with the big Rocket Space Ship.

When the perambulator was up in space safely coupled again to the big Astral Rocket Space Ship Marty began to chart the course on his instrument panel.

"Must inspect Martinean tower on Moon before return to planet Earth," he announced, and he pushed the proper button to blast the perambulator and the big Astral Rocket Space Ship out of the orbit around Xonia.

"Hey, Marty," said Willie, "do you think we'll have time to explore the Moon just a little bit before we blast off to go back to Earth?"

Marty consulted the timepiece on his wrist.

"Can explore Moon two minutes after inspect Moon tower," he said.

Within a short time the space ships were whirling around in the Moon's orbit. After Marty had uncoupled the perambulator from the Astral Rocket Space Ship by remote control, he blasted the perambulator out of the Moon's orbit. The Astral Rocket main ship continued to orbit the Moon.

Marty brought the perambulator down to a pinpoint landing on the Moon at the foot of the spidery Martinean tower with its blinking green lights.

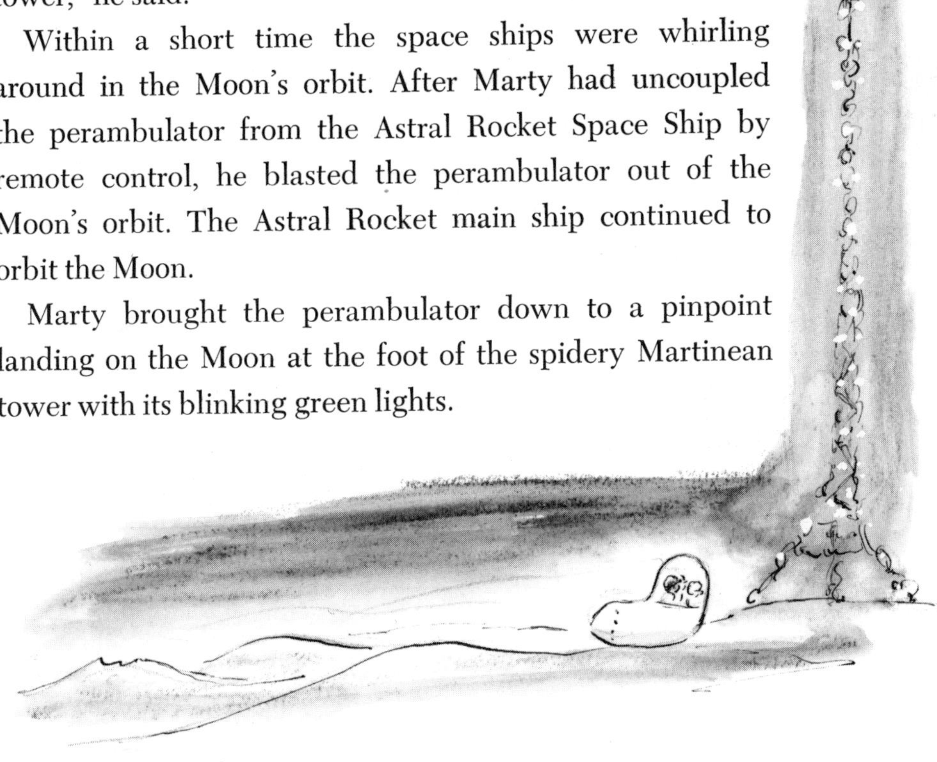

He reached down into a small locker underneath their seats and brought out some tightly folded clothes.

"This pressurized temperature-controlled Moon suits," he said. "Put on Moon suits."

Eddie and Willie managed with some difficulty to get into the Moon suits in the crowded little perambulator. Then Marty reached into the same locker and brought out three transparent helmets and two pairs of heavy Martinean space shoes. Willie and Eddie were surprised that the small locker could hold so much.

"Put on oxygenized pressurized helmet and space shoes," he said. "This necessary. No atmospheric pressure on Moon, no oxygen, very small gravity pull."

He put on one of the helmets and gave Willie and

Eddie the other two along with two pairs of space shoes. He was already wearing space shoes, as usual. And he didn't need a Moon suit because the Martinean spaceman's uniform he wore under his Boy Scout shirt was already pressurized and temperature-controlled.

Willie and Eddie had a harder time getting into their helmets and their space shoes than they had had with the Moon suits because the Moon suits they wore had puffed up as soon as they zipped them closed.

When they finally got the helmets and shoes on they were all so squeezed together in the small perambulator that when Marty opened the side door he was popped out like a pinched watermelon seed.

The boys clumsily climbed out of the perambulator after him. As they were adjusting themselves to the strange feeling of weightlessness and lack of atmospheric pressure on the Moon's surface, Marty was already busy inspecting the big Martinean tower.

He swiftly rocketed up and down and around the tower inspecting the struts and some of the complicated machinery on top of it. Marty wore space shoes that were equipped with miniature jet-propulsion engines in their thick soles.

Eddie had seen Marty and other Martineans on the planet Martinea flying around in their jet-propelled space shoes before. But Willie, who had never seen Marty or anyone else rocketing around in jet-propelled shoes, was surprised and he gaped at him with his mouth open.

Marty's inspection of the tower was over soon and he rejoined Willie and Eddie on the surface of the Moon.

"Tower work good," he announced, and then after he looked at the timepiece on his wrist he said, "Now explore Moon two minutes before blast-off to planet Earth."

He spoke through a small speaker in the front of his transparent helmet and Willie and Marty were startled when his amplified voice came into their helmets through receivers that were placed near their ears.

"Boy, oh boy, that must have been some job," said Eddie, "building that big tower up here on the Moon."

Marty nodded.

"Hey, Marty, how come the United States astronauts didn't see this tower when they were orbiting the Moon?" asked Willie through his speaker. "Yeah. And why didn't they see Xonia when they were orbiting on this side, the dark side of the Moon? How come?"

"United States astronauts no wear visualizers," said Marty. "Must wear visualizers to see Martinean tower and to see planet Xonia."

Willie had forgotten that he was wearing visualizers ever since he had put them on in the Central Park Zoo.

Marty impatiently looked at the timepiece on his wrist again.

"Now explore Moon!" he repeated sharply.

"O.K., Marty," said Eddie. "Where we gonna explore? Why not explore over where the U.S. astronauts landed?"

"Yeh, man, how about that, Marty?" said Willie. "That's a good idea."

Marty shrugged his shoulders and nodded. The only thing that interested him on the Moon was the Martinean tower that extracted material from the center of the Moon for making Zurianomatichrome . . . and beamed Secret Power Z to Martinea. The rest of the Moon held no interest for him.

He led the way back to the space-ship perambulator. Willie and Eddie followed him. He pushed the button that blasted them off the Moon surface and sent the perambulator rocketing around to the other side of the Moon.

They landed near the United States flag that they had seen when they orbited the Moon for the second time.

They climbed out of the perambulator and shuffled and hopped around in the moon dust (it was easier to hop, the Moon's gravity was so weak). They inspected some of the contraptions the American astronauts had left on the Moon. Marty studied them carefully. He would look at one, poke it around with his finger, then shrug his shoulders and sneer a little sneer and go on to inspect the next one.

It worried Eddie when Marty shrugged his shoulders. He was afraid Marty would dislodge the oxygenized, pressurized helmet that was clamped to his shoulders. He knew Martineans needed oxygen just as much as Earthlings do. Marty could lose oxygen out of his helmet as he

shrugged his shoulders, and then . . . Eddie shivered to think of what would happen with Marty overcome because of lack of oxygen, and he and Willie stranded up there on the Moon with a space ship neither one of them knew how to operate. He wondered how long they would last.

He looked at his wristwatch because he was anxious for these two minutes on the Moon to pass. His wristwatch had stopped!

Willie was not worried about anything. He had hopped about and inspected the contrivances the American astronauts had brought to the Moon until he saw a nice little flat stone in the moon dust. It gave him an idea. He picked up the stone, sat down near the pole of the American

flag, and got to work on the surface of the stone. He scratched into it with his Boy Scout knife.

At last the two minutes were up and Marty said through his speaker:

"Time now to blast off Moon. Ten seconds."

Marty and Eddie started to hop toward the perambulator. But Willie still sat in the moon dust near the flagpole and happily went on scratching on the surface of the flat stone.

"Hey, Willie, Marty said it's time to blast off," said Eddie.

"Just . . . one more second," said Willie slowly. Then he gave the stone one more scratch. "Now that's done," he said.

He stood up and showed Eddie and Marty the stone he had been working on. He had scratched into its surface a message that may very well be included some day in the world's history books about space exploration.

This was the message:

Willie placed the stone with its message at the base of the pole that held the flag of the United States.

They all hopped over to the space-ship perambulator and quickly squeezed themselves into the little ship. With some difficulty Marty slammed the door of the perambulator shut. The boys started to undo the clamps that held their transparent, oxygenized, pressurized helmets to their shoulders. But Marty shook his head.

"No take off helmets," he said through the speaker on his helmet.

He turned a lever on his instrument panel and the boys saw a bluish mist blowing into the perambulator from a vent on the panel. After a moment Marty said:

"Now oxygen and atmospheric pressure in space ship fixed. Take off helmets."

He went on to explain that since there was no oxygen or atmospheric pressure on the Moon the interior of the perambulator had lost its oxygen and atmospheric pressure when they opened the perambulator door. Now that had been fixed.

It was even more difficult to get out of the helmets and Moon suits in the crowded space ship than it had been to get dressed. Everybody's elbows were jamming into everybody else's eyes. Everybody's knees were butting into everybody's ribs.

But they finally got out of the Moon suits, helmets, and space shoes and Marty tucked them all away in a little locker under their seats once more. At last Marty was ready for the blast-off. He wiggled some gadgets on his instrument panel, pushed the proper button, and Z-O-O-M, they were up in space in time to rendezvous and couple with the big Astro Rocket Space Ship as it whirled around into the dim light at the edge of the dark side of the Moon.

When Marty had safely maneuvered the space ship past Earth's man-made scientific contrivances that orbited the Moon and they were out in clear open space, he pushed the proper buttons and switched the proper levers and set the controls on the automatic chart.

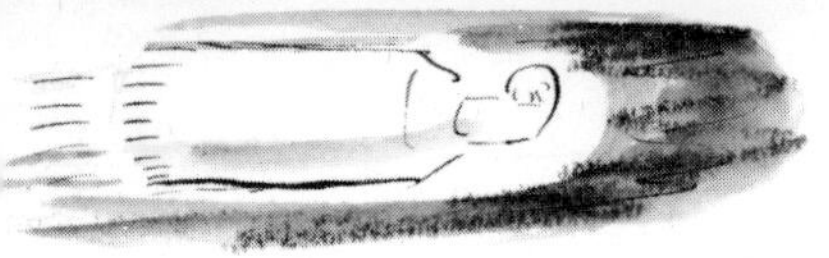

"Next stop Park Central Zoo, New York City," he announced, and leaned back.

They rocketed through space in silence for a few minutes, each with his own thoughts, until Eddie said:

"Hey, Marty, how come you . . . er . . . the Martinean scientists didn't have to change the direction of the Moon beam that was sending Secret Power Z to Martinea and touched Xonia?"

"Not necessary to change direction," said Marty. "Moon beam lose no power when passing corgi hill on Xonia."

"Well, man, am I glad of that. So the little dogs will have their biscuits," said Willie. "Those corgis are the prettiest dogs I ever saw. Hey, Marty, what's the right time? My watch stopped."

Eddie knew his watch had stopped too. He wondered if that happened because of the low gravity conditions on the Moon, or if it was the fine Moon dust that got into the works.

Marty studied the timepiece on his wrist for a moment. Had one of his remarkable Martinean machines failed him too? No, Marty was just taking his time and doing some figuring.

"Time now six o'clock P.M. eastern standard time, United States of America," he said at last. "Return pinpoint landing Park Central Zoo, New York City, 7:57 P.M. eastern standard time, United States."

"Six o'clock!" moaned Willie. "No wonder I'm hungry. Man, am I hungry!"

Marty looked sideward at Willie. He reached over and touched a small white button on his instrument panel . . . and said nothing.

"Man, oh man, I could eat a . . . What's that smell?" said Willie. "It smells like . . . it smells like baked beans, all dripping with molasses, and hot buttered biscuits! Man, oh man."

"Yeh, that smells good," said Eddie. "Where's that smell coming from?"

Marty busied himself doing things on his instrument panel.

The boys just leaned back and enjoyed sniffing the delicious aroma of baked beans dripping with molasses . . . and hot buttered biscuits.

"Hey, Eddie," said Willie after a few minutes, "I'm not hungry anymore. Funny, I feel as if I had me a good supper of beans and beaten biscuits, all buttered up."

"Yeh," said Eddie, "me too. I'm sort of full too."

Marty leaned forward and touched the white button on his instrument panel again. The delicious smell of well-cooked food was gone.

"Hey, Marty, what was that?" asked Eddie. "What was that smell? How come we're not hungry any more?"

"This latest Martinean scientific experiment," said Marty proudly. "Concentrated nourishment vaporized . . . now concentrated food in vapor, for long-distance space travel. All necessary proteins, carbohydrates, vitamins."

"Man! You mean we ate our supper just smelling it?" cried Willie.

Marty nodded.

"Wish there had been some ketchup on my beans," grumbled Eddie. "I like ketchup on beans."

Marty said nothing but kept his eyes glued to his instrument panel.

The rest of the journey back to Earth was uneventful. Willie and Eddie were drowsy from the big meal of baked beans and biscuits they had sniffed up from the concentrated nourishing vapor. They fell asleep and did not wake up until Marty shouted:

"Hold breath for landing!"

And the satellite space-ship perambulator plunged down to a gentle pinpoint landing in the wooded dell in back of the old brick building that had been the lion house in the zoo in Central Park, New York.

When they landed Marty climbed out of the space-ship perambulator with Willie and Eddie for just a minute.

They remembered they were still wearing the visualizers, the rose-colored glasses Marty had lent them before they blasted out of Central Park. They gave the visualizers back to Marty and they also returned the supersonic Sonambulator rings, the defense weapons Marty had lent them on Xonia.

Marty shook hands with both of them, a good, strong, special Boy Scout handshake. As he was shaking Eddie's hand he pointed with his other hand to two tiny new silver buttons on the collar of his spaceman's uniform.

"I now complete First-Class Martinean Scientist Explorer," he whispered confidentially.

"Boy, oh boy, Marty," exclaimed Eddie, and he pumped Marty's hand up and down to show him how glad he was. "Boy, oh boy, why didn't you tell me that before?"

Marty didn't answer. He lowered his eyelids modestly

and blushed. His ears became fiery red. Then he quickly said:

"Good-bye, good friends."

And he jumped into his space-ship perambulator and blasted off with a Z-O-O-M to return to his home in distant Martinea.

Willie and Eddie watched the small space ship disappear into the rosy summer sky. Now, of course, it just looked like a flying ice-cream cart, because they no longer saw it through Martinean rose-colored visualizers.

They waved at the ice-cream-cart space ship until it became just a tiny dot . . . and then it was lost in the setting sun. They silently walked back to the house where they both lived on Amsterdam Avenue.

11. On the Stoop

EDDIE and Willie sat on the front stoop of the house. It was the day after Marty blasted off to return to his home in Martinea. There were no other people around so they talked in low voices about their trip to Xonia and about their friend Marty.

"What a man, what a man," said Willie, "that Marty sure is. But Eddie, some of the stuff he talked about . . . was that for real?"

"What stuff?" asked Eddie.

"I don't know. I wonder somtime if he was just putting us on," said Willie. "I mean, like Xonia being the smallest planet in the Universe. Listen, I read about some small planets . . . well, there's one called Eros. Now there's a planet that's only about thirty-five miles long and it's floating around out in space in our own galaxy . . . right now!"

"Marty only said Xonia was the smallest *inhabited* planet in the Universe, remember—the smallest planet with living creatures on it," said Eddie. "Now that could be."

"Yeh, I suppose it could be," said Willie. "But what about the Martinean scientists believing the Moon broke off the Earth, and Xonia broke off the Moon, and stuff like that? That's what the man said."

Eddie nodded.

"Now, Eddie, that's a pretty old scientific idea," said Willie. "There're new ideas about the beginning of things . . . oh, something about . . . Well, there was this great big whirling hot mass of gases and burning hot rocks see, and it was whirling and whirling and whirling around in space until things began to sort of tighten up and the Earth was formed, and other planets and the Moon and maybe even Xonia. That happened billions of years ago and things cooled down and then living things began to grow. Well, I'm not too sure about the ideas but the new ones go something like that."

"Yeh," said Eddie slowly, "that could be. I know Marty and the Martinean scientists sometimes make a mistake, but most of the time . . ."

"Now listen, I don't mean he's not the greatest," said

Willie hastily. "He is, and even if he misses sometimes he's the biggest little man I ever saw."

"Yeh, he sure is," said Eddie quietly.

"Eddie, lookit . . . here's something I'd like to know," said Willie. "Whose idea was it to let the Xonians go on using the Secret Power . . . you know, from the Moon beam from the tower . . . I mean for growing things and feeding the little dogs? Was that the idea of the Martinean scientists or was that Marty's idea? You know what I mean?"

"Well . . . yeh. I think," said Eddie slowly, "I think that was Marty's idea and the Martinean scientists let him do it."

"Yeh," said Willie, "I think so too. Man, he sure is the greatest."

"Yeh," said Eddie. "He sure is."

And they sat there in silence again for a few minutes thinking about their friend Marty. After a while Eddie asked:

"What did you tell your mother?"

"She didn't ask me," said Willie. "She wondered why I didn't want any supper. I just told her I was full of beans and biscuits. A friend of mine treated and I wasn't hungry. What did you tell your ma?"

"She didn't ask me anything either," said Eddie. "I ate a little supper and I told her we went exploring up on some hills but we didn't see much. There wasn't much to see."

They sat there quietly for another minute. Eddie thought of the many good adventures he had had with his friend Marty in the past summers ever since he first met Marty and his space ship under the apple tree in his grandmother's orchard.

"Do you think he'll ever come back?" asked Willie.

"Who?" said Eddie, lost in his own thoughts.

"Who? Marty, that's who!" said Willie. "Yes, sir, he's quite a man, that Marty. I sure do wish he comes back sometime."

"Yeh, Marty's quite a man," said Eddie, and he sighed. "But I guess he'll never come back to Earth again now that he's a first-class Martinean Scientist Explorer. Maybe he'll go exploring on planets even farther away from his own planet Martinea than the Earth. And I bet he'll discover things and see things that no one ever saw or heard of before . . . even on Martinea."

"Yeh, maybe he will," said Willie thoughtfully. "Maybe."

And they both sat there quietly and said nothing.